W9-BYM-562

*Talkative Man*

# ALSO BY R. K. NARAYAN

# Talkative Man

## A Novel

## R. K. NARAYAN

Elisabeth Sifton Books
VIKING

ELISABETH SIFTON BOOKS • VIKING
Viking Penguin Inc.
40 West 23rd Street,
New York, New York 10010, U.S.A.

First American Edition
Published in 1987

LIBRARY OF CONGRESS CATALOGING IN PUBLICATION DATA
Narayan, R. K., 1906–
Talkative man.
I. Title.
PR9499.3.N3T3   1987   823   86-45387
ISBN 0-670-81341-9

Printed in the United States of America by
The Book Press, Brattleboro, Vermont
Set in Bembo

They call me Talkative Man. Some affectionately shorten it to TM: I have earned this title, I suppose, because I cannot contain myself. My impulse to share an experience with others is irresistible, even if they sneer at my back. I don't care. I'd choke if I didn't talk, perhaps like Sage Narada of our epics, who for all his brilliance and accomplishments carried a curse on his back that unless he spread a gossip a day, his skull would burst. I only try to interest my listener or listeners, especially that friend Varma who owns The Boardless Hotel. (He is considerate, keeps a chair for me inverted in a corner so as to prevent others from occupying it, although from the business point of view I am not worth more than a cup of coffee for him, whenever I stop by.)

My chair was generally set facing a calendar portrait of that impossible demon Mahishasura with serpents entwining his neck and arms, holy ash splashed on his forehead and eyeballs bulging out through enormous side-whiskers, holding aloft a scimitar, ready to strike. I never liked that picture

. . . too disturbing. It was a seven-year-old calendar, ripe to be discarded, but Varma would not hear of it. He would boast, "I have never thrown away any calendar for thirty years. They adorn my walls at home, sometimes four on a nail, one behind another. All our Gods are there. How can anyone discard God?"

It was no use arguing with that man Varma; he was self-made, rising from a menial job to his present stature as the proprietor of The Boardless, which fact proved, according to him, that he knew his mind and could never be wrong. I never tried to correct him, but listened, even appreciatively, to his spasmodic reminiscences. Fortunately he was not much of a talker, but a born listener, an ideal target for a monologist: even while counting cash, he listened, without missing a word, as I sat beside his desk and narrated my story.

★ ★ ★

The story that enchanted Varma was the one about Dr Rann, which I told him off and on spread over several weeks.

Dr Rann was actually, as I discovered later, Rangan, a hardy Indian name which he had trimmed and tailored to sound foreign; the double N at the end was a stroke of pure genius. One would take him to be a German, Rumanian or Hungarian – anything but what he was, a pure Indian from a southernmost village named Maniyur, of the usual pattern: tiled homesteads and huts clustering around a gold-crested temple that towered over an expanse of rice fields and coconut groves; similar to a hundred others, so commonplace that it escapes the notice of map-makers and chroniclers.

From this soil arose Rann of double N. He had blonde hair, a touch of greenish-blue in his eyes, and borderline complexion – unusual for an Indian of these parts. My private view on his ethnic origin might sound naughty, but is quite an historic possibility. A company of British, French or Portuguese soldiers must have camped at Maniyur or in its vicinity in the days when they were fighting for colonial supremacy and, in the intervals of fighting, relaxed by philandering among the local population.

I met him for the first time at the Town Hall reading room. Those were the days when I was struggling to establish myself as a journalist. They used to call me Universal Correspondent since I had no authority to represent any particular publication. Still, I was busy from morning till night, moving about on my bicycle or on my neighbour Sambu's scooter. I was to be seen here and there, at municipal meetings, magistrates' court, the prize distribution at Albert Mission, with a reporter's notebook in hand and a fountain pen peeping out of my shirt pocket. I reported all kinds of activities, covering several kilometers a day on my vehicle, and ended up at the railway station to post my despatch in the mail van with a late fee – a lot of unwarranted rush, as no news-editor sat fidgeting for my copy at the other end; but I enjoyed my self-appointed role, and felt pleased even if a few lines appeared in print as a space-filler somewhere.

I did not have to depend on journalistic work for

my survival. I belonged to one of those Kabir Street families which flourished on the labours of an earlier generation. We were about twenty unrelated families in Kabir Street, each having inherited a huge rambling house stretching from the street to the river at the back. All that one did was to lounge on the *pyol*, watch the street, and wait for the harvest from our village lands and cash from the tenants. We were a vanishing race, however, about twenty families in Kabir Street and an equal number in Ellamman Street, two spots where village landlords had settled and built houses nearly a century back in order to seek the comforts of urban life and to educate their children at Albert Mission. Their descendants, so comfortably placed, were mainly occupied in eating, breeding, celebrating festivals, spending the afternoons in a prolonged siesta on the *pyol*, and playing cards all evening. The women rarely came out, being most of the time in the kitchen or in the safe-room scrutinising their collection of diamonds and silks.

This sort of existence did not appeal to me. I liked to be active, had dreams of becoming a journalist, I can't explain why. I rarely stayed at home; luckily for me, I was a bachelor. (Another exception in our society was my neighbour Sambu, who, after his mother's death, spent more and more of his time reading: his father, though a stranger to the world of print, had acquired a fine library against a loan to a scholar in distress, and he bequeathed it to his successor.)

I noticed a beggarwoman one day, at the Market Gate, with Siamese twins, and persuaded my friend Jayaraj, photographer and framer of pictures at the

Market Arch, to take a photograph of the woman, wrote a report on it and mailed it to the first paper which caught my attention at the Town Hall reading room; that was my starting point as a journalist. Thereafter I got into the habit of visiting the Town Hall library regularly to see if my report appeared in print.

The library was known as Lawley Memorial Library and Reading Room, established on a bequest left by Sir Frederick Lawley (whose portrait hung from a nail high up near the ventilator) half a century ago. An assortment of old newspapers and magazines was piled up on a long table in the middle of the hall, mostly donated by well-wishers in the neighbourhood. Habitual visitors to the reading room sat around the table on benches, poring over newspaper sheets, not noticing or minding the dates on them. An old man sat at the entrance in a position of vantage and kept an eye on his public. He had been in service from time immemorial. He opened the doors precisely at nine in the morning and strictly closed them at five in the evening, shooing off the *habitués*, who sometimes stepped in the opening and stayed on. "Fortunately," said the old man, "the Committee won't sanction candles or lanterns, otherwise those loungers would not leave till midnight." He was intolerant and suspicious of most people, but tolerated me and, I could say, even liked me. There was a spare seat, a wooden stool at his side, which he always offered me. He admired my activities and listened to my city reports, and hoped I'd find some donors to subscribe for current newspapers. I managed to get some money from

Varma himself, though he was resistant to all approaches for money, that enabled us to get two morning papers from Madras.

Today when I entered the Reading Room, I found my usual seat occupied, and the librarian looked embarrassed. A man dressed in full suit was sitting on my stool. He looked so important that the librarian, as I could see, was nervous and deferential, which he showed by sitting forward and not leaning back with his legs stretched under the table as was his custom. He looked relieved at the sight of me, and cried, "Here is a man waiting for you." The other made a slight movement, acknowledging the introduction. I threw a brief glance at him and decided he was an oddity – dressed as he was in a blue suit, tie, and shining shoes, and holding a felt hat in hand. He sat without uttering a word. Somehow, I resented his presence and suppressed an impulse to say, "Why do you sit there dumb? Say something and above all quit my seat. I am not used to standing here." The newspaper addicts at the long table were watching us, so unused to seeing anyone in a blue suit and hat in the Town Hall. The old librarian was fidgeting, unable to attend to his routine work.

I fixed my look rather severely at the stranger and asked, "You wish to talk to me?"

"Yes," he said.

"Then come out," I said. "We must not disturb the readers." I felt triumphant when he rose to his feet and followed me to the verandah. I surveyed the prospect before me with authority and declared to my companion, "Not an inch of space for us to

6

sit," and then glanced at him from head to foot, and realised that the fellow was short — though while seated he looked imposing. "Not an inch," I declared again, "everybody is everywhere." Vagrants were stretched out on the lawn, fast asleep; idlers sat in groups cracking peanuts and popping them in. The cement benches scattered here and there were all taken.

"Let us step down and see," he said, looking about, trying to conceal his disgust at the spectacle of Malgudi citizenry. "How is it so many are asleep at this hour?"

"They must have spent a busy night," I said.

I began to enjoy his discomfiture and said, "Why don't we go over and sit in that shade?" indicating the southern corner where a spreading banyan tree stood with its aerial roots streaming down. He threw a glance in that direction and shuddered at the sight of more loungers in addition to a couple of donkeys standing still like statues, and mongrels curled up in the dust. He looked outraged at my suggestion. I added, "The grass is soft there," asking myself, What, did this man expect Spencer's Furnishing Department to provide him cushioned seats?

He simply said, "I am not used to sitting down. Lost the habit years ago."

"How long ago?" I asked, trying to draw him out, hoping he would become reminiscent. He ignored my question and asked suddenly, "Is there a bar or a restaurant where we may possibly find a quiet corner?"

I really had no idea still why he sought me, out of the hundred odd thousand populating our town.

The librarian must have given him a golden account of me. Why was that old man so fond of me? I suspected that he might be a match-maker and have his eyes on me as eligible for his granddaughter, me a bachelor with not a care in the world, owning property in Kabir Street.

"No bar or a good enough restaurant," I said and added, "nor do we have an airport or night club except Kismet in New Extension, not very good I hear. If you are interested I could give you a long list of things we don't have – no bars, sir, we have only toddy shops, which serve liquor in mud pots, which one has to take out."

"Not interested, thank you. I am a TT. I only order orange juice at a bar and seek a quiet corner for a chat."

"Nor are apples and oranges known here. We only come across mango, guava, gooseberry, all cheap fruits," I said, getting into a devilish mood and resenting more and more this man's presumptuous presence in our town. I was exaggerating its shortcomings, avoiding mention of Pasha's Fruit Stall at the northern end of the market, which displayed on its racks every kind of fruit. He was said to get his apples directly from Kulu valley, grapes from Hyderabad, dried fruits from Arabia, and so on. He won prizes every year for the best display of fruits at the market.

"When did you arrive?" I asked Rann when we had managed to find a vacant space on the fountain parapet. Two men had just moved away, and I grabbed their seats as if jumping out of a queue. He had no choice but to stoop down, blow off the dust,

8

spread his kerchief, and sit beside me on the parapet. After all these preambles I now left it to him to begin a conversation. He remained silent waiting for me to question him. After a few minutes, I remarked on the weather and went on to a lot of political tit-bits to prove that I wasn't taken in particularly by his blue suit.

"What did the old man tell you about me?" I asked.

"That you were the one person who could help me."

"What sort of help? I had no notion that I was so important."

"Don't say so, one can never judge oneself. You are a journalist, active and familiar with this town, and certainly would know what's what."

That won me over completely, and I asked, "Where are you from?"

"Timbuctoo, let us say."

"Oh, don't joke."

"No joke. It is a real place on the world map."

"Oh!" I said. "Never expected any real person to come out of it. You are the first one."

He became serious and said, "A lovely place on the west coast of Africa. A promising, developing town – motor cars in the streets, skyscrapers coming up – Americans are pouring in a lot of money there."

"May I know what took you there and what has brought you here?"

"I was on a United Nations project."

I didn't ask what. Project is a self-contained phrase and may or may not be capable of elaboration. I come across the word in newspapers and among academicians, engineers and adventurers. One might hear the word and keep quiet, no probing further. Sometimes a project might involve nothing more than swatting flies and sending reports to the headquarters.

He volunteered an explanation as if catching the trend of my thoughts. "I have to send a report to my headquarters out of the voluminous data I have collected. I am also writing a book on a vital theme. I learnt that this is a quiet town, where I may collate my material in peace. Here I have been the last three days, practically living in the little waiting room of your railway station. Oh! the bed-bugs there! I sit up all night for fear of them. Tell me, who is the railway minister now, and help me to draft a letter to him."

His presumptuousness annoyed me. Ignoring his question I hallooed to the peanut vendor hovering about with a bamboo tray on his head. When he came up I engaged myself in a game of haggling, disputing his measure and quality, before buying a handful of nuts which I kept on the parapet beside me. My friend looked rather shocked. I explained, "Full of protein, you know, packed and hermetically sealed by nature, not the minutest microbe can sneak in: you may pick the nut off the road dust, crack it open, and eat it without fear of infection. Don't you consider the arrangement splendid?"

I demonstrated my observation by hitting a nut on the cement surface to crack it open, and held it out to him. He shrank from it, mumbling an excuse.

★　　★　　★

The next duty he imposed on me was to bring him out of the railway waiting room. The station master was distraught. He was a diminutive person whose job was to flag in and out two passenger trains at wide intervals, the non-stop express, and the goods wagons. After each performance he re-rolled the flags, tucked them under his arm, and turned into his office to make entries in a buff register while the Morse keys tapped away unattended. After the passengers left, he put an iron lock on the platform gate and retired to his "quarters", a small cottage fenced off with discarded railway sleepers, besides a Gul Mohur tree in whose shade his children, quite a number, swarmed, playing in the mud. He was a contented man, one of the thousands apparently forgotten by the Railway Board in far-off Delhi. He still had two years' service before retirement, and then he would go back to his village a hundred miles away. It was a life free from worries or hurry until this stylish passenger alighted from Delhi. His blue suit and manner overwhelmed the little man, as he stepped out of a first-class compartment majestically.

The old porter thought, with some pride, Someone from London, and hoped for a good tip. The train moved. The porter tried to lift the big suitcase. The visitor said, "Waiting room," at which the porter looked embarrassed.

The diminutive station master noticed the scene and came running after completing his duties in his little office.

"You are in charge?" enquired the visitor.

"Yes, sir, I'm the station master," replied the man

with a touch of pride but restraining himself from adding, I've still two years to go and then will retire honourably, back to my village where we have our ancestral land, not much, four acres and a house.

"Where is the waiting room?"

"Over there, sir, but please wait, I'll get it ready for you."

He himself took charge of the suitcase from the porter, although he was only a few inches taller than what was really more like a wardrobe trunk, and hauled it along to the station verandah.

"Don't drag it, I'll carry it," implored the visitor.

"Never mind, sir," said the station master and would not let go his grip till he reached the verandah. The porter was gone to fetch the keys of the waiting room and also a broom, duster, mop and a bucket. Opening the door, the station master begged, "Don't come in yet." With the porter's help he opened a window, dusted and swept the room, and got it ready for occupation. He kept saying, "I've requisitioned for carpet and furniture at headquarters."

After a couple of days, he realised that the grand visitor had no intention of leaving. Dr Rann went out in the morning and came back only at night. It was against the rules to let anyone occupy the waiting room for more than two nights, but the station master was afraid to say so to the present occupant. Next time I visited the railway station with my letter for posting, the station master said,

"The Railways Act is very clear as to rules for occupancy of waiting rooms, but there is this man who wants to stay permanently. I fear I'll get into trouble – for thirty years I've served without a single adverse note in my service register – if the DTS ever stops for inspection, it'll be the end."

"How can he know how long the occupant has been –"

"Entries in the register."

"Don't make the entry."

"For thirty years I have lived without a remark in my service records."

"I'll ask him to buy a ticket for the next station, while waiting for the train. He can buy a ticket for Koppal, which will cost after all two rupees," I said. But, he looked miserable at the prospect of a doom after thirty years of unblemished service.

"Don't worry about it," I said finally. "Keep him for another day or two till I find him a place. I'm sure your DTS won't come in the near future. Even if he does, mention my name, and he will say OK."

I had the journalist's self-assurance although I did not have any paper or news editor to call my own. (The station master, I noticed, was too timid to ask my full name, knowing me only as a journalist.) He was busy fingering the telegraph keys.

"7 Down will be at the outer signal in a few minutes."

He got up and directed the porter to run up to the yard and release the signal. The train arrived, and a group of villagers returning from the weekly market fair at Koppal got off with their baskets, bags, bundles and children. I ran up to the mail van and handed in my despatch for the day, with the late fee. The mail sorter said, "Why do you waste money on the late fee, when you could post normally at the HO?"

"You may be right," I replied, "but I have to wait till the last minute for news. Anything might turn up at the last minute."

He stamped the envelope and the engine whistled and moved, while the station master stood flourishing the green flag. The porter went up to lock the signal lever.

I chose this moment to take out a five-rupee note and present it to the station master, with, "Just a goodwill token for the festival." I could not specify a festival, but there was bound to be one every day in the Hindu calendar. "We have 366 festivals for 365 days," said a cynic once. The station master was used to receiving such goodwill tokens from businessmen, who did not want their parcels to be held up in the goods yard and loaded on a later train. The station master looked pleased as he pocketed my five-rupee note.

I whispered, indicating the waiting room, "The one in there is no ordinary soul – he is from Timbuctoo."

The station master was duly impressed with the manner in which I delivered this news. He asked,

"Where is Timbuctoo?"

I did not know myself, so I said: "One of those African countries, you know . . . interesting place."

Between the bugs and the station master, Rann felt uncomfortable continuing as a resident of the waiting room. And for me the daily visit to the railway station for mailing my despatch was becoming irksome. The moment he flagged off the 7 Up, the station master would turn his attention to me; luckily, he would not immediately be free, as he always had something to write on those hideous buff-coloured forms, or had to give a couple of taps to the telegraph key in his office, all this activity taking less than five minutes. When he dashed into his office for this brief interregnum, I could dash out and escape, but when he found me trying to slip away, he gripped my arm and led me into his office. I fully knew his purpose – to talk about his waiting room occupant.

"Sir, you must think of my position – you must do something about that man there – he can't make this his home."

"Why do you tell me?"

"Whom else am I to tell?"

"How can I say? I'm not his keeper. Why don't you speak to him yourself?"

"I don't know how to speak to such gentlemen."

"A pity! I don't know how to speak to such gentlemen myself. I have not been taught."

He wailed, "I don't know how to approach him. He goes out, and when he comes back, he shuts himself in and bolts the door. Once Muni knocked on the door and was reprimanded severely. When he comes out he moves so fast, I can't speak to him at all."

"That's how they live in foreign countries – they always move fast and won't tolerate any disturbance except by previous appointment."

"Oh, I didn't know that," he said seriously.

Another day he wailed, "That gentleman was

angry this morning. He said he is going to report to the Railway Board about the upkeep of the station – you think I care? I have served for thirty years – I can ask for retirement any moment if I like. What does he think? Am I his father-in-law to look after him?"

"Definitely not," I said and he looked pleased at my concurrence.

"He is grumbling about bugs and mosquitoes as if the railways were cultivating them! The notions some people have about railways!"

Rann would buttonhole me in the Town Hall, where he knew my hours of visit. He also browsed among the musty ancient volumes in the back room, having gained favour with the librarian.

"I say, my friends – the bugs are eating me up every night. Do something. That funny man at the station says that it is not his business to keep the waiting room free of bugs and mosquitoes."

"May be that is the Railway Board's policy to discourage the occupants from staying too long."

"Should I write to the Railway Board?"

"No use, the bugs being a part of our railway service – they are service bugs actually."

"Oh, I didn't realise," he said, taking it literally.

"Anyway, why should you stay on there?"

It was the wrong question. "Where else can I go?" I shook my head, trying to evade any responsibility he might thrust on me. But there was no escape. He said, "I can leave the railway station only when you find me another place."

I ignored this proposal but could not suppress my curiosity. "How long do you have to be here?"

"I don't know," he said, "till my work is completed. I have to make a field study, collate and organise my material and write. I have found some rare reference volumes in the stack room of the Town Hall library – some early nineteenth-century planters' experiences and their problems, which give me priceless data for my study."

At my next visit to the station, the master cornered me again: "Impossible situation. This is the third week, your friend must go. He can't make the waiting room his father-in-law's house."

"Why not?" I bantered.

"I have told you a hundred times, rules don't permit more than eight hours' stay between trains, may be extended by a couple of hours at the discretion of the station master. Not more. I'll lose my job at this rate!"

"Why don't you throw him out? What have I to do with him?"

"Don't go on in this strain, sir. How can I treat roughly a big man like that?"

"Rules are rules and he may not be so big, after all."

"I have never seen anyone dressed like him!" the station master said reflectively. "I feel afraid to talk to him. I asked Muni to go up and tell him, but when Muni peeped in, that man turned round and asked, 'What do you want?' and Muni withdrew in confusion. Please help me get him out of here somehow."

I thought it over and said, "Keep him for a week or ten days on a ticket to the next station each day and I promise to pack him off or find him a room."

The station master looked doleful and began, "Thirty years' service —"

I held out twenty rupees and said, "You will buy him a ticket for Kumbum every morning and punch it for ten days and you will say he arrived by 7 Up or something, waiting to catch the 17 Down or whatever it is."

This proved effective. Whether he pocketed the money or bought the ticket each day was not my business to probe. That gave Rann ten days' extension.

I utilised the time granted to search for a room. It was proving an impossible task; Rann could not specify what he wanted. I took him around all over the town — east, west, north and south. I had no confidence to have him on the pillion of Sambu's scooter, so I thought it best to engage an autorickshaw. One had to make an advance booking for it — it was gaining such popularity among the citizens. One morning I set aside all my other business and went to Nalli's Hardware, owned by Gopichand, an astute businessman who had migrated from Sind during the partition. He said, "Take the auto at the stand if you find it. I never can say where they may be found until they return at night to give me the day's collection."

I drew myself up and asked haughtily, "Why should I come to you if I can find it at the stand?" My tone was indignant. I had served him in my own way — helped him to print his handbills when he started his autorickshaw business, brought him customers for his hardware, and also enlisted subscribers for a crazy financial scheme. He remembered my help and at once relaxed, "Anything for you, my friend. You are my well-wisher," and summoned his boy and said, "Go at once and find Muniswamy and come with the vehicle."

It was an idle hour for hardware business and he seated me on an aluminium stool and discussed politics. When we exhausted politics, I watched the crowds milling about the market, leaving Gopichand to read a newspaper reclining on a bolster amidst his hardy environ of nails and rods and chains and clamps.

The boy came back to say, "Muniswamy is away, can't be found."

Gopichand proclaimed grandly, "Tomorrow morning the vehicle shall be at your door. Very sorry to disappoint you today." As a compensation he drove the boy out to the next stall to fetch a sweet drink for me which came in an opaque unwashed glass. I declined at first, but had to pretend to drink in order to please him.

Next morning the autorickshaw was at my door.

"Ah, you have also started using an auto!" commented my immediate neighbour Ramu, who had grown so fat and immobile that he could do nothing more than sit on the *pyol* leaning on a pillar morning till night enjoying the spectacle of arrivals and departures in Kabir Street. I looked on him more as a sort of vegetation or a geological specimen than as a human being. He loved to play rummy, provided the company assembled around him.

Now he remarked from his seat that an autorickshaw ride was heating to the blood and also disjointed the bones. The autorickshaw driver Kari was upset at this remark and retorted haughtily:

"People are jealous and create such rumours. Simpson Company at Madras have built the body and they know what is good for our bones."

And he stepped out and approached Ramu to explain his point with vigour. I didn't like this development and summoned him back to his seat, hurriedly shut and locked the door of my house, and got into the rickshaw.

"Railway station," I commanded.

He started the auto and over its rattle said, "Did you hear what that fatty said, as if —"

I didn't encourage him to go on. "Don't you pay any attention to such things. They are all an old-fashioned, ignorant lot in our street."

"People are better informed in Lawley Extension. More enlightened men there."

"Naturally," I said, which agreement pleased him, and by the time we reached the station he was quite at peace with the world. I left the auto in the shade of the giant rain-tree outside the station, went up and found Rann half asleep in a chair in the waiting room. He stirred himself and explained: "Not a wink of sleep — what with bugs and mosquitoes and the rattling goods wagons all night."

"Get ready, we'll inspect the town. I'll wait outside."

While I waited, the station master sidled up to me and whispered, "DTS is coming . . ."

"You have already said that several times."

He lowered his voice and asked, "Does he drink?"

"How should I know?"

"He was wild last night, threatened to kick Muni for some small fault if his —"

"Never mind," I said indifferently.

"Please take him away before bad things begin to happen."

Rann was wearing olive-green shorts with his shirt tucked in at the waist, and crowned with a solar topee as if going out hunting in a jungle or on a commando mission. Actually, as we proceeded through the crowds in the Market Road he looked as if watching wild-life, with eyes wide open in wonder, and over the noise of the vehicle, he kept saying, "Never been in this kind of vehicle — a bone-rattler really . . ." (I prayed to God that Kari would not hear) and kept asking, "Where are you taking me?"

I felt irritated and ignored his question.

First stop was at Abu Lane, which was off the East Chitra Road. We pulled up in front of an old building. He cried, "Seems like a downtown area — not suitable."

"What's your downtown? Anyway we are not placing you here — stay in the auto . . . I'll be back."

He sat back sullenly while a small crowd of downtowners, old and young, stood around staring at the autorickshaw decorated with a pouncing tiger painted on its sides, and at the fantastic passenger. I dashed up a wooden stair in the verandah to a little office of a young real-estate agent, and picked up from his desk a list of available houses in the town, returned, and ordered Kari, "First drive to North-end."

"North-end? Where?"

"Across Nallappa's Grove, other side of the river."

"Oh, there! No houses there," said Kari.

"Twenty North-end, come on," I said with authority.

"Cremation ground there . . . no houses."

I flourished the list before his eyes. "That chap there who gave me this list knows the city better than you. Just drive on, as I say."

Rann seemed to be affected by the term cremation and began to fidget. "Let us try other places. . . ."

"Don't be scared. Hey Kari, don't talk unnecessarily . . . go on."

One of the men watching obliged us with the statement, "The cremation ground was shifted further off."

"But the corpses are carried that way, the only way to cross the river — even two days ago —" Kari began.

But I said, "Shut up, don't talk."

"I don't want to live on that side of the river," said Rann.

"Why are you sentimental?" I asked.

It was getting stuffy sitting in that back-seat and getting nowhere, with time running out. Rann began to narrate something about his days when he had to carry on his field studies with dead bodies strewn around. "One gets used to such things . . ." he concluded grandly while the crowd stood gaping at us. I said determinedly, "Driver, North-end. Are you going or not going? We have not set out this

morning to parade ourselves in this street . . .
wasting our time . . . Rann, come out."

He edged his way out and both of us stood in the
street unused to so much publicity.

"Follow me," I said. "We'll find some other
means of going."

"Now where are we going?" he asked.

"Follow me, don't go on asking questions like a
six-year-old urchin."

He was cowed by my manner, and followed me
meekly, with the locals forming a little procession
behind us. I really had no idea what my next step
was going to be. I had a general notion to go to
the Market Place and complain to Gopichand
about his driver or seek the help of Jayaraj to get
a vehicle. Perhaps a *jutka*, but I was not sure if
Rann could crawl into it and sit cross-legged. I
was so grim that no one dared talk to me while I
strode down the road without any clear notion of
where I was going. The autorickshaw followed at
the tail end of the procession. He honked his horn
and cleared a way through the crowd and drew up
alongside.

"Who pays the meter charges?" Kari asked.

I glared at him and said, "Your boss Gopichand.
I'm going on foot so that he will know what sort of
a service he is running in this city with you as his
driver. And with this distinguished person, whose
feet have never touched the street!"

There was a murmur of approval from the
assembly moving with us.

Someone came forward to confront Kari and say,
"You fellows deserve to be . . . to make a foreign

gentleman trudge like this . . ." That settled it. Kari felt humbled and contrite.

"I never said anything to upset those masters. They themselves got out of their seats."

And the busybody said, "Forget and forgive, sirs. Get into your seats." I took this chance and accepted his advice and pushed Rann into his seat, sat down, and said grandly, "North-end first."

An hour later we reached North-end over a broken causeway at Nallappa's Crossing. I had the satisfaction of noting water splashing off the wheels on the green uniform. Rann looked disconcerted but said nothing, bearing it all with fortitude. We arrived at North-end: a few thatched huts and, beyond them, an abandoned factory with all the windows and doors stolen, leaving gaping holes in the wall. Away from the factory four cottages built of asbestos sheets with corrugated roof, meant for the factory staff, stood in various stages of decay, and all passage blocked with anthills and wild vegetation.

I was a little shocked that the real-estate agent should have this first on his list. The young agent must have taken someone's word on trust and placed it on his list. Not a soul anywhere. We didn't even get down. Dr Rann smiled wanly. I said, "These things happen, you know. Now Kari, turn round. The next on our list is . . ."

Kari looked quite battered by the strain of driving his rickshaw. Our eardrums were shattered, so were our joints. The man from Timbuctoo began to droop and looked bedraggled in his safari olive-green, which had now lost its original starched neat gloss, and revealed damp patches at the armpits and at the shoulders; the jacket was unbuttoned, exposing a grey vest underneath. If our expedition had gone on further, I'm afraid he would have stripped himself completely. This was the second day of our search, with no time left for tiffin or lunch. Yet I saw no end to our quest. We had our last trial at New Extension, a bungalow bearing the number 102/C. The auto stopped at the gate. The house looked fresh and promising. Rann surveyed it through the gate railings and declared, "It'll be a nuisance to maintain the garden – and what should I do with a big house?" He shook his head without even waiting to inspect it. A caretaker came running, opened the gate and said, "I've the keys."

Rann was unmoved: "I don't want a big house."

"Not a small house, nor a medium-sized one, not on the East or West, North or South, neither downtown nor uptown," I said singsong, carried away by the rhythm of the composition. I tried to sound light-hearted but felt bitter, and hated the whole business of house-hunting.

We got into the carriage. On the way back, I saw the kismet, and stopped.

"Come in, I want to celebrate the non-conclusion of our expedition with ice-cream and coffee. Normally I'd have preferred The Boardless, but it is miles away at the other end – and I am not sure of being able to bear up that long."

Rann brightened up. We refreshed ourselves. I ordered coffee and snacks to be sent out for Kari too, who had borne the brunt of our house-hunting and was waiting patiently outside. When the bill was brought Rann's fingers fumbled about his safari pockets. But I held up a warning sign grandly and paid down, although it was four times what it would have cost me at The Boardless. I belonged to the Kabir Street aristocracy, which was well known for its lofty, patronising hospitality, cost what it may.

The moment we reached the railway station, the station master came up to tell me, while Rann had gone in, "Message has just come that the DTS arrives at 17 hours tomorrow for the day's inspection. Your friend must positively vacate right now. I have to tidy up." There was no choice. As soon as Rann appeared, I asked, "How many pieces have you, your baggage, I mean?"

"Not many. Why?"

"Pack them up at once. You have no time to lose. If the DTS arrives anytime now, you will have to live in the open. Pack up and be ready and come out in thirty minutes. That's all the time you have."

"Outrageous. Where is that funny man the station master? Where are you taking me?"

"Don't become difficult or questioning, unless you want your baggage thrown out. The DTS has authority to throw out things you know."

The station master stayed out of sight, but I was sure he was listening. I said to Rann finally,

"I'll leave now, but send the rickshaw back for you and your bags . . . I'm too tired to answer more questions. You have no choice – unless you want to take the next train to Madras."

"Oh, no, that can't be done . . ."

★    ★    ★

When he arrived at my door with his heavy suitcase

26

and an elegant roll of sleeping bag and other odds and ends, the whole of Kabir Street was agog. People stood at their doors to watch the new arrival.

Malgudi climate has something in it which irons out outlandish habits. It was not long before the blue Oxford suit was gone – perhaps embalmed in moth-balls; and the doctor began to appear in shirt-sleeves and grey trousers, almost unrecognisable. In due course even that seemed odd and out of fashion in a street where everyone was seen in a dhoti from waist down edged with a red border over a bare body, or utmost in a half-sleeve shirt on occasions. For a few weeks Rann used to come out only in his three-piece suit puffing and panting in the heat. At home he would never emerge from the privacy of his room except in pyjamas and a striped dressing gown tasseled at the waist. Luckily I had inherited a vast house, no stinting for space as I have already mentioned. So vast and uninhabited, you'd be in order even if you wore no clothes when you emerged from your room; but here was this man, who never opened his door without being clad in his robe, his feet encased in slippers and a heavy towel around his neck.

We were not familiar with this costume. On the first day, the old sweeper who had been coming to clean and dust since the days of my parents gave one startled look at the gowned apparition emerging from the front room, dropped her broom, and fled to the backyard, where I was drawing water from the well, and said, her eyes wide open, "A strange man in that room!" And the stranger was equally startled, and retreated like a tortoise into its shell, shutting the door behind him. He could not shut himself in indefinitely, however he had to visit the toilet in the backyard.

I had to tell him that I could not change that century-old architecture in any way. He was aghast at first that he would have to travel all the way from his front room through two courtyards and corridors to wash and perform his ablutions at the well. But I gradually trained him, repeating every time, "Where there is a will . . ." The latrine was a later addition, with a septic tank which I had installed after coming into possession of the property. On the very first day I had to explain to him a great deal, rather bluntly:

"You will have to accept this as it is. I cannot change anything – I can't bother myself with all that activity even if I find the time, money and the men."

Following it, I gave him a tour of inspection of the house. When he saw the flush-out latrine he said:

"This is impossible. I have no practice – I need a European type –"

"In that case you have come to the wrong place. Our town has not caught up with modern sanitary arrangements, even this is considered a revolutionary concept. The *Modern Sanitaryware* man on Market Road is going bankrupt – sitting amidst his unsold porcelain things. Our ancestors bathed and washed and cleansed themselves at the well and the river. With the river running down our door-step, they didn't have to make special arrangements, did not let themselves be obsessed with washing all the time, which is what Western Civilisation has taught us.

Considering that the river flows almost all the year round, although thinning down a bit in summer —" I waxed eloquent and left him no choice.

"What do I do with the bathrobe?"

"Oh, don't worry about too many details. Things will sort themselves out. I'll drive a peg into the wall, where you can hang down your robe."

★   ★   ★

"What does that word Timbuctoo sound like?" I began an article. "It's a fairy-tale or cock-and-bull setting. Sometimes a word of disparagement or . . ." I went on for about a hundred words in the same strain, and finally came down to the statement, "Hereafter we must pay more respect to that phrase. For I realise today that Timbuctoo is very real, as real as our Malgudi. I have actually shaken hands with a man from Timbuctoo. You will be right if you guess that I poked his side with my finger to make sure that he was real. . . . He has come on a vital project on behalf of the UN and it's an honour for Malgudi that he should choose to work here. From his description of the place, Timbuctoo is a paradise on earth, and you feel like migrating, abandoning our good old Motherland." And then I composed a word picture of Rann in his three-piece suit.

Every journalist has his moment of glory or promising glory — the brink of some great event to come, a foretaste of great events. A knock on my door, and my neighbour stood there outside, the fat man who rarely stirred from his seat on his *pyol*. This massive man held out a telegram.

"This came when you were away . . . I signed the receipt."

While I tore it open, he waited to be told of its contents. I looked at him, murmuring a word of thanks, and wishing mentally that he would take his massive self off. Oh, big one – be off! I said mentally. I had much to think and dream over the message in the telegram, which was from my editor: "News item interesting – but useless without a photograph of the Timbuctoo Man. Get one soonest." For the first time in my life I was receiving encouragement. Normally whatever I mailed would be lost sight of, like flotsam on the current of Sarayu in flood. Or if it was printed, it would be so mutilated and presented in such minute type that you would have to search for it with a magnifying glass; and of course, no payment would be expected for it, not that I needed any, thanks to the foresight of my forefathers, who did not believe in spending but only in hoarding up endlessly. Here was the telegram in my hand, and this enormous man would not leave so that I might dream on it.

I turned to go in and he said, "Hope all's well? Good news?"

"Oh yes, excellent news – from my news editor who wants something written up – routine stuff." I sounded casual and tried to turn in, even as the fat man was saying, "I'm very nervous when a telegram arrives. Otherwise I'd have opened it to see if it was urgent, and then of course, I'd have gone in search of you." The picture of this paunchy man with multiple folds shuffling along Market Road barebodied in search of me was too ridiculous, and I burst out laughing, and shut the door, murmuring, "Very kind of you."

I gloated over the message secretly – not yet decided how far I could share the feeling of journalistic triumph with others. I went about my day feeling that I was on the brink of a mighty career. I don't aspire to become a so-called creative writer, I kept saying to myself, but only a journalist who performs a greater service to society, after all, than a dreamy-eyed poet or a story-teller. The journalist has to be in the thick of it whatever the situation – he acts as the eye for humanity.

Sitting in my corner at The Boardless lost in thought, my coffee was getting cold, which was noticed by Varma in spite of his concentration on the cash flow in the till. He suddenly ordered, "TM's coffee is getting cold. Boy, take it away and bring hot." I woke from my reverie to explain:

"A telegram from my editor, important assignment – but it depends very much on a photograph. . . ."

"Whose?" he asked.

"I'll tell you everything soon." I left it at that. Didn't want to make it public yet. I brooded over it the rest of the day and decided on action – since it was urgent and could be a turning point in my career – I must be ready to go anywhere if ordered, even if it meant locking up my home in Kabir Street. But I had misgivings about Rann, doubts about his reaction to a photo. Some instinct told me that it would not be so simple. And my instinct proved reliable when I faced him with the request. He was in his room. When I sounded him out, he became

31

wary, and asked: "Why?"

"Just for the fun of it . . . You have lived in many countries and must have interesting photographs."

He brushed aside the suggestion with a wave of his hand, and resumed the study of the papers on his desk. Remarkable man. Though I had given him an unfurnished room, he had furnished it with a desk and chair and a canvas cot. I hadn't entered his room till now – he always locked it when leaving for his bath. He had been getting about evidently.

"How did you manage to secure a desk?"

"On hire. I found a shop on Market Road . . . for the four pieces they will be charging fifteen rupees . . . not bad, less than a dollar and a half, that's all – very cheap . . ."

Rather disconcerting. He was entrenching himself while I had thought of giving him only a temporary shelter. I asked in a roundabout manner:

"How much advance for the whole period?"

He was evasive, "Well not much really by world standards. He'll collect the hire charges from time to time, and no time-limit."

He was too clever for me. I left it at that, looked around the walls and said, "No photographs?"

"What sort of photograph?" He shook his head. "I don't like photos of any sort."

"I thought you might have an interesting collection, having lived in so many parts of the world . . ." I sensed this man would not give me his photograph. Today he was wearing a Japanese kimono and looked grim and busy.

"I must get these reports off – already overdue – all this amount of travelling is unsettling and interferes with one's schedule."

I rather resented his continuing to be seated while I stood. I was consumed with curiosity to know what the report was about; there was a pile of typed and handwritten sheets. Where were the reports going? But I let the queries alone. My immediate need was for a photograph of this man. Some instinct told me not to mention it now.

I consulted Jayaraj later. "I want a photograph of the man. . . ."

"Put him before my camera and you will have it."

"But he seems to shy away from the camera – I do not know why. Otherwise I could invite him to have a group photo with me as a mark of friendship."

"I'd charge twenty-five for photographing two figures . . ."

Following this I got into a pointless debate which in no way concerned the present problem. "So does it mean that if you take a group photo of fifty school children you will count the heads and charge *pro rata*?"

"Naturally," he answered. "How else? I have to survive. If you find another photographer, you are welcome to go to him. Can't get rolls, either 35 or 120, no developer, no printing paper – hopeless situation. I think our government is trying to suppress photographers, and they draft their import rules accordingly. The little supply I have are thanks to that helpful breed called smugglers, who come regularly to that coastal village at Kumbum, their country craft loaded with things – where I go once a month to buy materials. The bus fare is five rupees each way, and I have to recover it in the charges to my customers. The Councillor came for a frame of a wedding group. I told him point blank that he was welcome to bring anything to frame, but no photo business please. Nowadays I am concentrating more and more on framing pictures and the painting of signboards — but even there . . ." He went on haranguing an imaginary audience about the conditions; frames that were flimsy, cheap wood, dyed and passed off as gilt frames by the suppliers, which once again was due to government policy. He was obsessed with the wiles of a hostile government out to do him in. I always allowed plenty of time for his speech, while sitting comfortably on the bench which jutted out of his shop at the Market Entrance. The authorities did their best to remove the bench, as it obstructed the public passage, but could do nothing about it, and Jayaraj always boasted that he would go to the Supreme Court if necessary to keep his long bench where he chose. His fundamental right could not be questioned.

He talked on squatting on the floor, his hands busy nailing and cutting frames; in a recess at the back wall he had his photographic department — that mysterious darkness where he professed to have treasures of photographic equipment through the grace of his friendly smuggler. After allowing him as long a speech as he desired, I said,

"Be a good chap. My whole career depends on your help now. I'll manage to bring that man this way, and you must manage to snap him, front or side, without his knowledge, and enlarge it. We want only a bust."

"Done," he said readily. "My camera is the old type, on a tripod, but the best ever made, I can't take a snap with it, but I'll get the Japanese one from the Councillor who got it from the smuggler recently, which I can hold in my palm, and work wonders with the telephoto lens and superfast film."

He got into the spirit of adventure and stood up at the entrance of his dark room and said, "I can stand here and click when you step into that arch. But tell me the precise date and hour when you propose to bring him. I'll do anything for a friend who remains undiscouraged by what I may say."

"Of course, I know that – otherwise wouldn't I try the Star Studio?"

"That wretched fellow! Don't go near him. He is a photographer of propped up corpses – no good for live subjects."

He approached his task with a lot of seriousness. He brooded over the logistics. He held a sort of dress rehearsal next morning with me understudying for Rann. In this season sunlight fell aslant at a particular spot under the Market Arch for about twenty minutes, but as the sun rose higher there was a shade . . .

"I must catch him in full light while it is available – otherwise I may have to use a flash, which is likely to put him off. Five minutes, that's all. You must see that he faces the market and stands still for a moment. I'll see to it that no one crosses in at that time. I'll post my boy to keep people away, only for a few minutes and no one will mind it either, not a busy hour. . . . It'll be up to you to see that he doesn't pass through without stopping. Perhaps you should hold him and point at something. Don't worry that you may also be in the picture – I'll mask you and blow up the other."

He leapt down, marked the spot for me under the arch, directed me to look straight ahead, hopped into his shop, concealed himself in the dark room, and surveyed through the viewfinder. I'd never expected he would plunge so heartily into the scheme.

"You should be a film director," I said.

I fell into an anxious state. The rehearsal was very successful but the star would have to cooperate without knowing what was going on. And he could be manoeuvred only once, there could not be a retake. I was pressed for time – the newspaper might lose interest if the photograph was delayed. Jayaraj could borrow the smuggled Japanese camera only for a day from the Councillor. I'd have to catch hold of Rann and manipulate him through. It was nerve-racking. In order to think I had to retire, to what used to be known in our family as a meditation room, a sort of cubicle in the second court, away from the general traffic routes of the family where you could retreat. It was dark and musty with a lingering smell of stale incense, a couple of pictures of gods faintly visible in the sooty wall. There I retired so that Rann might not intrude. A blue glass pane among the tiles let in a faint sky light, enough for my purpose. I sat down on a wooden plank, cross-legged, and concentrated on my problem, with a scribbling pad on my lap. I jotted down a script for the scene ahead.

*Evening today:* 1. Meet Rann and describe the Swami's Cottage Industries at the market as worth a visit. Talk him into it. (*Earlier* prepare Sam to be ready with a souvenir for Rann.) Explain to Rann that Sam is one who respects international personalities, and always invites them to honour him with a visit, and that he has collected and treasured letters of appreciation from outstanding men. Rann must spare a little time for my sake. *10.10 a.m.* Leave Kabir Street and walk down. *10.25 a.m.* Market Arch. Stop and push him gently towards the foundation tablet now covered with grime. Encourage him to scrutinise the inscription. *10.30 a.m.* Leave Arch.

Rann fell into the trap readily. I knocked on his door and saw him lounging in my canvas chair, my heirloom, and wool-gathering. He was probably feeling dull. So it was a propitious moment for me to make the proposal.

"Can you spare half an hour for me tomorrow morning?"

"Well, of course, what for?"

"You have been here and not known the peculiar treasures of this town."

"I'm so preoccupied with my work. . . ."

"I know, I know, but still you must look around. You will find it worthwhile . . . I want to take you to meet a friend of mine in the market."

"Market! It'll be crowded."

"Not always. I'll take you at a time when it is quiet. I want you to see a handicrafts shop – a very small one, managed by a chap we call Sam – absolutely a genius, dedicated. He makes lacquerware and sandalwood stuff which are famous all over the

world. So many awards at Leipzig and other international fairs. He has distributors in Africa, Europe,
the US and everywhere. He is well known all over
the world; mainly foreigners come in search of him
and place orders. He is less known here as usual.
No visitor from a foreign land ever misses him.
Their first question will always be, "Where's *Sam's
Crafts*?" Ten o'clock tomorrow morning we will
walk up; spend half an hour at his workshop and
then you will be free. He will feel honoured by a
visit from an international figure."

The scheme worked according to timetable. At
the Market Arch I paused, he also paused. I stepped
aside. I pointed at the fading tablet on a pillar facing
us and as he stood gazing at it, I was aware of the
slight stirring of a phantom at the threshold of
Jayaraj's dark chamber. I kept talking.

"It's mud-covered, but if you are keen we may
scrape the mud off and see the date of the foundation
stone . . ." He stood gazing at it and said,

"Thanks, don't bother about it . . ." and we
moved on to Sam's.

★   ★   ★

I had gone as usual to post my news at the mail van
when my friend the station master came to see me,
all excited, saying,

"There is a large woman who came by 7 Down,
staying at the waiting room and won't leave, just
like the other fellow, that London man whom you
took away – perhaps you should take away this
woman too."

"None of my business, whoever she may be," I said.

38

"Not my business either." he said. "The waiting room is not my ancestral property to be given to every –"

Before he could complete the sentence, the subject of his complaint was approaching – a six-foot woman (as it seemed at first sight), dark-complexioned, cropped head, and in jeans and a T-shirt with bulging breasts, the first of her kind in the Malgudi area. She strode towards us, and I knew there was no escape.

"You must be the journalist?" she asked menacingly having observed me at the mail van. She took out of her handbag a press-cutting of "Timbuctoo Man", with the photograph of Rann I had managed to get.

She flourished the press-cutting and said, "You wrote this?"

"Yes madam," I said meekly.

"No one can fool me," she said.

The diminutive station master tried to shrink out of sight, simpered and stayed in the background. I felt rather intimidated by the woman's manner, but still had the hardihood to retort,

"What do you mean by it?"

"I mean," she said undaunted, "if you know where this so-called doctor is, you will lead me to him."

"Why?"

"For the good reason that I am his wife – perhaps the only one wedded to him in front of the holy fire at a temple."

I took time to assimilate the idea.

"Of his possibly several wives I was the only

one regularly married and the first. You look rather stunned sir, why?"

"Oh no," I said clumsily. I had no other explanation. The whole picture of Rann was now assuming a different quality if this lady was to be believed. The station master looked embarrassed but, held by curiosity, hovered about with the rolled flags under his arm, and behind him stood the porter. We were the only ones on the railway platform. She eyed them for some time without a word and then asked,

"Station master, is your work for the day over?"

"Practically – 9 Up is not due until 20 hours."

"What's 20 hours? Now the bother of addition and subtraction," she muttered. "Why don't you railway people use a.m.–p.m. as normal civilised beings do?"

"Yes madam," he said sheepishly.

"Is that your only porter?" The porter, on being noticed by the queen, came a few paces forward.

"I've served here for thirty years, madam," he said. The queen accepted his statement without displaying any special interest, whereupon he withdrew a few paces back, but within hearing distance. She swept her arms about and said,

"Normally, they'd have a couple of cement benches on any railway platform, but here nothing. Come on, let us go into the waiting room – anyway, there at least are a couple of chairs. Come! Come!" she said beckoning me authoritatively. Sheepishly I followed her. She had a commanding manner.

The station master followed discreetly at a distance. She carried two chairs out of the waiting room. "No, no," I persisted, "let me –"

But she would not pay any attention to my gallant offer and said, "You have seen him, tell me all about him."

"I cannot say much . . . Ours was a brief meeting. I was interested because –" She did not let me complete the sentence:

"It is more important for me to know where he is rather than anything else."

She looked so fixedly at me that I said, "Not in my pocket," and tried to laugh it off. "We met for less than fifteen minutes at our Town Hall library where he had come for a reference work and did not like to be interrupted."

"So studious indeed! How marvellous! Good to know that he is still bookish." And she laughed somewhat cynically. Then she became serious and said, "All that I want to know is where is he at the moment. If you will only give me a hint I'll give you any reward."

I felt slightly upset and said righteously, "I'm in no need of a reward. I can survive without it." The station master, who was following our dialogue from a respectable distance, added,

"He is rich, madam, come from a big Kabir Street family really."

She said, "Station master, perhaps you would like to attend to other things?"

The station master shrank out of sight, and the porter too melted away. I got up saying, "I must go now, you must excuse me. The only novelty about

him was his mentioning Timbuctoo, and as a
journalist I thought it had news value. After that I
lost sight of him, never asked him where he was
going – that's all. He was enquiring about some long
distance buses ... That's all madam, all that I can
say is that if he is staying in this place, he cannot remain unnoticed." I had given full rein to my im-
agination. "I'd suggest you look for him at Madras
or a place like that instead of wasting your time
here." And I rose, carried my chair in and said,
"Goodnight." I felt uncomfortable in her presence
with a constant dread lest I should betray myself. And
so I hurried away, glancing back over my shoulder to
make sure she was not following me. She stuck to her
chair without a word and watched me go.

★   ★   ★

Rann was in his kimono when he opened the door,
on my knocking repeatedly, with a scowl on his
face. I resented his attitude: in my own house he
was a visitor to whom I'd offered asylum for no
clear reason. It had just been an impulse to help him,
nothing more, and to rescue him from bed-bugs
flourishing in the railway station waiting room. Yet
he behaved as if I were a hotel steward violating the
privacy of a guest.

"Why don't you hang a 'Don't disturb' board on
your door? I thought you might have brought a
souvenir from one or the other of the hotels in your
travels –"

He was taken aback. "Why do you·say that?"

"I see that you are busy –" I said cynically. He
wasn't. I could see that he had been lounging on the

canvas easy-chair (my heirloom) which I had let him have out of idiotic kindness. Yet this man dared to shut the door and look too busy to open it. There were no papers on his table, nor a book at his side in the canvas chair or anywhere. He must have been lounging and staring at the ceiling and wool-gathering, and he chose to scowl at me – me, his saviour from bed-bugs. Soon my anger was mitigated as I anticipated the pleasure of shocking him with news I knew his flamboyance and foreign style would be punctured. I simply announced, from the door, like the opening lines of a play, "A lady to see you," and turned round, shutting the door behind me (a piece of deliberate good manners). I went down to the backyard and shut myself in the bathroom and stayed there, although I had heard him open his door and follow me. I took my own time.

When I opened the bathroom door, he stood there, his face full of questions, and he seemed to have become a little paler and shrunk a few inches into his Japanese kimono. I had not needed a wash, but I had splashed water over my head for no better reason than to taunt him. "Oh!" I cried with feigned surprise. Then I raced along the back courtyard to my room, while he followed me. My clothes and things were widely scattered in various rooms in different blocks of that house, and I never found at any time what I wanted, towel in one room, kerchief in another, trousers at another corner, and so forth. Now I was dripping, water running over my eyes, and wet all over – very annoying. I cried, "Where is the damned towel?" At which Rann vanished for a minute and fetched a fresh towel from his room. I felt pleased with my show of authority, murmured a thanks indistinctly, and wiped my face and head. We were standing in the passage.

"I'll return it washed tomorrow —" I said.

"Oh, that's all right," he said. "No hurry."

"So soft and strong," I said admiringly and stretched it and held it to the light from the courtyard. I noticed an embroidered corner and spelt out 'Neville'.

"What's that?" I asked.

"Hotel in Rhodesia — it's a souvenir." Perhaps he had stolen it.

"How long were you there?"

"Oh, quite a few times in connection with the project —"

"But they say, it's difficult for coloured people —"

"Oh, it's all exaggerated. Don't you believe it. For me, no problem, the UN Passport can't stop you anywhere."

I felt inclined to provoke further elaborations on the subject, while I knew he was dying to ask questions about the lady but feeling rather awkward about reviving the subject. I felt a sudden compassion for him — his bewilderment and awkwardness as he shrank into his fancy kimono. I asked suddenly, "You want to ask about that lady?"

"Yes, yes," he said meekly with a sigh, "I don't understand it at all. Who is she?"

"The station master says that he saw a photograph in her hand, looking like your good self."

"Ah!" he cried involuntarily.

"It matches the picture in the *Telegraph*."

"How did my photo get in anywhere?"

"Newspapers have their sources, you know."

He asked, "What sort of a person is she?"

"Well, a long time ago I gave up staring at women and studying their worth, so I'm not able to provide a good description. Anyway, I'll dress and come to your room, please wait there."

He was waiting impatiently in his room. I had taken my own time to look for my clothes, to groom myself before my mirror, the ornate oval in a gilded frame with a vine pattern carved on it, perhaps a wedding present for my grandmother: it was full of spots and blank areas. Now fresh from an unnecessary bath and dressed in my *kurta* and a laced *dhoti* and a neatly folded upper cloth over my shoulder, I felt ready to face the emperors of the earth. I strode into his room, where he had had the good sense to leave the door open. I had a glimpse of him fidgeting impatiently in his chair. The moment he saw me he rose and offered me the seat, and lowered himself into it only after I had sat elsewhere. Now I looked as if ready to go on with our conversation and give him a hearing.

"I told you about a lady at the railway station where I had gone to post my evening despatch."

I knew that Rann was dying to have a description of the lady as he sat squirming and fidgeting.

"Was she tall?" he asked, trying to draw me out.

"Could be," I replied.

"Medium height?"

"She did not seem short," I said. "I could see her only from a distance."

"How far away were you?" he asked stupidly.

I felt irritated. "I forgot to take a measuring tape

45

with me," I said, and tried to laugh it off. He looked miserable and I had to ask,

"Why are you bothered?"

He said, "Because – I don't know. You are right. Dozens come and go at the railway station, do I care?"

"Bravely said," I remarked. "Let us go to The Boardless. You will feel better."

He shrank from the idea. He had, apparently, a fear of being waylaid by the woman. I persuaded him, but before coming out, he spent much time to decide how to dress for the visit. I advised, "The Boardless is a special place, where you could go in your underwear or in royal robes, it's all the same to the crowd there. No one will question or notice." Still, he took his time to decide and came out in a pink slack shirt and grey flannel trousers.

We walked up. I took him to my usual corner, facing the Mahishasura calandar, had another chair put up. The habitués turned round to study him for a moment and then resumed their coffee and talk. I ordered *dosai* and coffee, but he couldn't enjoy it; he seemed overwhelmed and self-conscious. Varma, the proprietor, said "Hallo" to him formally and looked gratified that The Boardless should be attaining an international touch with this man's visit. I briefly explained, "He is a scholar, come on business" avoiding Timbuctoo because of its phoney sound. I thought I should do something to integrate this stranger in our society and cure him of his kimono and carpet-slipper style and alienation, and so had persuaded him to walk along. Of course, it had not been an easy passage though, people stared at us – it was inevitable.

\*     \*     \*

The lady's haunting presence at the railway station somehow drove Rann closer to me. He seemed to depend on me in some obscure manner for any information I might spring on him. He looked on me, I suppose, as a possible harbinger of some good news such as that the lady had left suddenly by some train or that she had thrown herself under the midnight goods train. So he watched my movements eagerly with almost a questioning look to say, "Any good news? How good is the goods train? Anything under it?" Formerly, he had always shut himself in his room and bolted the door. These days he kept a door open so that he might not lose glimpse of me; while I moved about he watched me surreptitiously from his chair, which was an excellent position for spying. My forefathers must have used that same strategic position to keep an eye on the household, particularly the army of servants, so that no one could slip out unnoticed. Rann found this advantageous. As I passed in and out he greeted me with casual ease. "Good day to you, TM. Starting on your interesting rounds for the day?" Sometimes he just smiled and nodded, without obviously questioning, feeling perhaps: "If he has anything — he is bound to tell me — not the sort to keep mum —"

On the whole, he seemed to have limbered up, and was slightly more relaxed. It suited me, too. I took advantage of his leniency and the half-open door policy to step into his room informally for a chit-chat now and then. I'd walk in and make straight for the easy chair without any preamble.

★　　★　　★

47

I lounged in his canvas chair comfortably. He sat in his hired chair uneasily, pretended to be looking through some papers on his desk, put them away, and got up and paced the narrow room up and down like a bear in the cage. After a pause and silence for fifteen minutes I just pronounced,

"You seem very agitated, why?"

"Oh, no. I am sorting out some problems in the paper I'm writing."

"Very well then, let me leave you in peace . . ."

"No, no, stay," he said. It seemed to me that he wanted to say something but was reluctant to begin or rather unable to find an opening line.

"I do not mind relaxing and lounging here all day, but you will have to do something about it — about the lady in question," I said.

"What do I care? Hundreds of persons come and go at a railway station."

"Not everyone carries your photo asking questions —"

"What the hell!" he cried red in the face. I enjoyed the annoyance he displayed and added,

"Also calls herself your wife."

"Nonsense!" he cried, and paced up and down. I had never found him in such a mood or using intemperate language. The thought of this woman seemed to unloosen the bolts of his mental framework.

"What's he to Hecuba or Hecuba to him?" I asked light-mindedly.

"Does she call herself Hecuba? I knew no one of that name."

I had to explain to him that I was quoting Shakespeare.

"Ah, Shakespeare. I had almost forgotten. Long time ago, of course. Would you believe it? Once I sat down and read the Oxford Edition from the title page to the last."

"Yet, thou varlet weakeneth at the mention of a perfidious female!"

"I say, this is maddening! Please do something and send her away."

"Why? This is a free town for anyone to come and go or stay. How can I arrogate to myself any right to expel anyone! I don't think I'll see her again . . ."

"What's she like?" he enquired suddenly. I couldn't continue in a mood of levity – if she was really his wife. So I just said,

"Well, an impressive personality – slightly dark, but a commanding personality, rather large build, I should say. Perhaps exaggerated by the blue jeans and T-shirt and bobbed hair. The station master was quite cowed by her manner and opened the waiting room promptly when asked . . ."

"Though he made such a fuss when I wanted it! That funny character. Did she mention her husband to him also?"

"I don't know," I said, "but he was the first to be shown your photograph."

"Outrageous!" he cried. "You have done me a disservice!"

"On the contrary I was doing you a service without being asked. Do you know the number of men who curry my favour to get their names in print?"

"You could have at least consulted me!"

"It'd be against the journalists' code. Freedom of

49

the Press and all that. Even the PM cannot say 'Yes' or 'No' to a journalist when he is out to make his copy," I said grandly.

"Photograph! How did the photo get in?"

"I can't say – you have been in so many places, anyone might have snapped you."

After about an hour's rambling talk he begged, "Don't betray me. You have been hospitable right from the beginning, just help me now by leaving me alone and without mentioning me to that person whoever she may be, in jeans and T-shirt. Is she Indian? I'll explain everything when the time comes. Not now. Don't ask questions."

"After all," I said, pitying his plight, "she is not going to live permanently in the waiting room. She will have to leave some time. Don't be seen too much for some time," I said encouragingly.

"I need a lot of mental peace at least till I complete my work. That's why the shelter or asylum you have given is doubly valuable. I must have no sort of distraction till I complete the writing of my book. Anyone who helps me to work in peace will be my benefactor. To me nothing is more important than the book. It's going to be a sensation when it comes out. It will shake up the philosophers of today, the outlook will have to change. It's in this respect that I value your hospitality and shelter. When I publish I'll acknowledge your help surely."

"Ah ha, my name too will be in print. Excellent! While my profession is to get a lot of people's names in print, that is the first time it will be happening to me. Great! Do you know my name? You have never gone beyond calling me TM or UC as those people at The Boardless do – why not we adjourn to The Boardless for refreshments, after all you have visited it only once. I'm hungry."

He resisted the suggestion.

"Are you afraid to come out?" I asked and left it at that.

"Why should I be afraid? The world is full of evil things. I have seen all sorts of things, everywhere in this world. I'm not afraid of anything. Any airline hostess or a waitress in a restaurant might turn round and blackmail you if you were foolish enough to have said 'How do you do?' in a friendly tone. These are situations which develop unasked. I won't be disturbed too much by these things."

"So, a man of experience! Come out with me and if you are accosted, draw yourself up and say, 'Begone phantom wretch! I know you not.'"

"You are very Shakespearean today," he commented. I was happy to see him thawing. "I've also as I told you read Shakespeare with genuine pleasure," he added.

I decided to protect him from wifely intrusions.

★   ★   ★

How she found her way to Kabir Street must forever remain unexplained. There she stood on my threshold one afternoon. The neighbours viewing her from their *pyol*s must have been startled; her dress and deportment were so unusual in our setting. She was attired like a Punjabi woman, *kurta* or *salwar kameez* or whatever they call it, which seemed to exaggerate her physical stature, which was already immense. She was a large woman by any standard.

In our street where women were used to glittering silk sarees, gold and diamonds, she looked like a visitor from another planet. She wore around her neck white beads in a string, like a gypsy, and had around her shoulder a pink muslin wrap — the total effect was startling, really. No wonder the spruce tailor's dummy called Rann quailed at the very thought of her. I was happy that the fellow had gone out, and I only prayed that he would not blunder in and stumble on her. I seated her with her back to the window opening onto the verandah as you came up the steps so as to prevent her catching sight of Rann if he happened to come.

I didn't know where he was nowadays. I thought he went out to do research, but later learnt from our gossip sources what he was actually doing. I'll come to that later.

Now the big lady was settled squarely in the hall. I had placed her strategically so that she could have a view of the second courtyard and the crows perched on the roof-tiles and the drumstick tree looming beyond, and not notice Rann if he should appear on the other side of the window.

"I'm sorry, I've nothing to offer . . . this house is just a shell, I go out to eat — not a soul anywhere."

I refrained from questioning how she had managed to come. I guessed the station master must have given her directions.

She said, "I don't expect anything from you except help to get at that man."

I remained silent, not knowing what to say, dreading that she might turn her head at the sound of footsteps. She was there to investigate thoroughly.

"That station master is helpful . . . good man. But for him I'd have taken the next train back instead of continuing in this wretched place – Oh, the bugs in the waiting room!"

"Yes, yes, others also run away on account of it . . ." realising how similar Rann's experience was. That seemed to be their only common bond. (Bug-bond was the phrase that kept drumming in my head.)

"I gave him five rupees and he has been so helpful – even got a spray pump and eliminated the bugs almost fifty per cent! Now it is tolerable. He has also arranged to send me food from his house," she said.

Why is that fool of a station master so helpful, I wondered. Must warn him.

"He must be having special regard for you. Usually he applies the rules and won't let anyone occupy the waiting room for more than a few hours."

"Yes, he mentioned something, but five rupees goes a long way; first thing in the morning after 7 Up or 6 Down or whatever it is passes, I slip the five-rupee note before he can mention the rules and his unblemished service record in the railways. Also a couple of rupees to the porter, who sweeps and cleans the room and does not let anyone approach it – and so there I am. No one except yourself has set eyes on the so-called Rann for years. You must help me get at him . . . a strange character. Sometimes I have felt like wringing his neck but on the

53

whole I'm very very fond of him, although I am not sure what I'll do if I set eyes on him. Anyway, first show him to me and then I will decide." She tightened and bit her lips — her expression was so forbidding that I shuddered at the picture of slippery Rann in her grip.

"How did you get his photograph? He was always shying away from photographs. Even our wedding photograph he tried to destroy but I saved it. I have it with me in my box at the station."

"Why so?"

"Because he was a crook and wanted to remain invisible, that's all." She said this without hesitation. I didn't explain how I got the photograph because I feared she might call me a crook too, being so un-inhibited and loose-tongued. She suddenly went on, "Now tell me all about him. Though I loathe him, I like to hear about him."

I didn't see why I should oblige her with in-formation and so just said, "I too met him only at the Town Hall where I had gone to look at a paper. I stopped by because he was rather strange-looking in his three-piece suit and all."

She laughed at the mention of his suit. "Oh, three-piece suit. Three-piece suit! What a gentleman! Once he was one hundred per cent Madrasi — only *dhoti* and *khaddar* half-arm shirt."

"One could easily take him for a London banker now."

"Three-piece suit indeed! What shade?"

"Blue — all blue or near blue," I said, getting into the spirit.

"Tell me about him, I'm dying to hear all about

him . . . ages since I saw him, years and years, what does he look like? Has he grown stout? Your photograph doesn't say much."

"Newspapers won't print more than a bust or the head as on a coin or postage stamp, and that seems to have brought you down."

"If you had published a full photograph, that might have brought quite a crowd to your railway station, enough to drive the station master crazy."

"Must have been a popular man," I said.

"A regular lady-killer, sir; the only one who could survive was myself. I've been to the capitals of the world, hunting for him with the help of the Interpol and met only the poor wrecks he left behind when he vanished. What does he look like these days? Has he put on weight?"

I realised presently that like the Jesting Pilate, she would not wait for an answer. If I remained silent, still she would go on –

"He was quite attractive in those days. Does he have a moustache?"

"Yes, a thin line – reminds one of – reminds one of Adolphe Menjou, a film actor in the thirties –"

"Must be greying, surely . . . or does he colour? I wouldn't put it past him."

I remained quiet, letting her talk on. It looked as though I'd have to surrender my title of Talkative Man and take a second place in the world of talkers. My constant fear was that the fellow might arrive. I was apprehensive as to how they would react to each other, also about my position as his keeper. The lady would unhesitatingly call me a liar and might even assault me, which would create an unprecedented sensation in Kabir Street. She looked as if she might make a move. She must have heard rumours of my hospitality toward Rann — again from the station master.

On an idea, I got up with an excuse to go out: "I'll be back in ten minutes, suddenly remembered something . . ." I went down the steps to the fourth house in the same row, Sambu's. As usual, he was reading in his small study.

"Look, when Rann comes back to return your scooter, keep him here, lock him away if necessary till I sound the all-clear. Tell him someone is waiting for him — he'll understand."

After that I hurried down to the corner shop and bought a dozen bananas, a packet of biscuits, and a couple of soft drinks, went home, and set them on a plate before the lady.

"Ah, you are a thought-reader. Very welcome."

She must have been starving. She ate three plantains, half a packet of biscuits and washed it all down with a soft drink that claimed to be pure orange juice. Revived, she remarked, "Husband-hunting is a fatiguing business."

"Are you sure we are referring to the same person?" I asked.

"No doubt about it. The photograph is un-mistakable: he might make himself into Adolphe Menjou or whoever, or grow a beard or a horn on his head, but he can never change. Eyes and nose betray a man unmistakably. They cannot change or cheat. I have done nothing but gaze on his wonderful countenance for months and years out of count, and I know."

She paused and wept a little. I tried to look away, and did not know what would be the right statement to make in this situation. It was awkward. I did the best I could under the circumstances, looking away through the window – hoping and hoping that the man would not come back suddenly, bypassing Sambu or because the bookworm Sambu should forget to hold him, as was likely with bookworms. I contemplated this possibility while glancing at her mopping her tears with a minute handkerchief which she had to fish out of her bag each time, and wondered if it would be appropriate to lend her the "Neville" towel Rann had given me. Suppose she was settled here for the day? – since my parlour was as good as the waiting room for her. In a voice thickened with nose blowing, she said, "If I had the slightest clue that he would act like this ... At Madras, I was reading at St Evans in Egmore, and lived with my parents in one of those sidelanes nearby. My father had a furniture and carpentry shop and this man you call Rann would often come in on a bicycle; he was a delivery boy for a circulating library, delivering and collecting magazines, mostly film journals, charging a daily fee. He was also a student at Loyola College, supplementing his income through his job, which he seemed to enjoy, as it suited his wandering temperament. The library had a few journals of a serious kind in addition to film magazines, which appealed to my youthful taste in those days. He enjoyed his job because he could read all sorts of things, some of the serious journals too like the *National Geographic*. Occasionally he would recommend a special article in a journal to

57

improve my mind. He reserved his visit to us as the last on his rounds – bringing us the cheap magazines we liked as well as the serious ones which he would recommend us. In addition to delivering magazines his boss would send him to get racks and stools and benches for his shop from my father's workshop, which was a small shed in the backyard, though he employed many hands and turned out a lot of furniture for the shops around. A stone bench under a mango tree in our compound was very convenient for us. We sat close to each other, while he read out of a journal something that he felt I should know and understand. You know how it is when two young persons sit close to each other and discuss intellectual matters in soft whispers! Inevitable, inevitable . . ."

At this moment I noticed Sambu coming up my verandah steps. I excused myself for a moment and went outside. Sambu whispered: "That chap is come – about an half-hour ago – and is restless. What shall I do?"

"Kick him up a ladder to that loft in your hall and remove the ladder. He had better stay out of view for a long time. There is someone in there waiting to dismember him; I'll tell you the story later. She shows no sign of moving, but I'll do something about it soon. Please wait, and tell the idiot not to peep in at the window."

Sambu, an ever obliging neighbour, threw a brief glance at the window and withdrew.

I had to explain to the lady, "I'm afraid I've a meeting to report. My friend is waiting. I suggest that you go back to the railway station. I'll meet you in your room later when I come to post a letter in the mail van – after that I'll be free. You must also want to eat and rest. I'll definitely see you?"

*    *    *

She narrated her life story further, after ordering a couple of chairs to be placed under a tree on the railway station platform. She ordered the station master about and commanded the porter unreservedly until they supplied all her needs. I had posted my despatch dutifully – a court case and a municipal meeting, in the 7 Up to Madras. The platform was deserted; only the station mongrel lay curled up on the signalling platform. The lady had rested and looked refreshed and had now changed to a cotton saree, which made her look larger than she seemed in the morning. A mild breeze was blowing from the mountains, some birds were chirping in the tree.

"The waiting room must have been a dungeon at one time where prisoners were cooped up. I'd not want even my worst enemy to come in there. This tree is my shelter all through the day. I watch the travellers come and go and would willingly sleep under it during the night, but for my sex – still the world is not an easy or safe place for us."

I resisted the impulse to blurt out, Who would dare to come near you?

As if reading my thoughts she said, "I always carry a little pistol – of course licensed, because I'm an officer in the Home Guards at Delhi, though I have never had to shoot even a fly. I took a rifle-training course the police once organised at Madras, and I know which is the right end of a gun." And she laughed. She seemed to be in a benign mood now, having probably got it off her chest in the morning. "There is no train till 21 hours, to use the master's language – I think it is the 11 Up, a lumbering goods train which is so noisy that you can't sleep till it has passed the outer signal. You see, I'm picking up the railway language quite successfully."

After a few more pleasantries of this kind, she paused to look at the station master and the porter, standing respectfully a short distance away, and said, "That'll be all for the present, master. Tell your wife not to go to any trouble tonight. All I'll need is a glass of buttermilk if she can manage it."

"Definitely, madam," said the master and withdrew, followed by his porter. "I'll be away to do some marketing, madam, not more than an hour."

"Away till 17½ hours?" she asked with a laugh.

"Very much earlier," he said. "Muni will be here and will attend to any important messages . . . he's experienced." At which the porter looked pleased.

"I don't wish to bore you," she said to me, "but I have to tell you. In addition to our meetings in the evening at my home, he used to waylay me on my way to or from school and take me on his bicycle – I began to miss my classes happily, and spend the time with him at a coffee house or ice-cream parlour. He was very liberal in entertaining me. I was charmed with his talk on all sorts of subjects. Our discussions on the cement bench under our mango tree became infrequent since we were together in other places. We went to the museum, where he would take me through, explaining all sorts of things. I liked his voice and felt thrilled to be told about the eleventh-century bronzes or in another corner about the nomads or forest tribes and their cowrie-shell ornaments, and so on. And of the stuffed animals, their habits and character, whatever he said would just charm me. I couldn't decide how much of what he explained was genuine – but it held me, his voice lulled my senses. The museum was the nearest rendezvous for us, and I could go back home from there unnoticed, but sometimes we took the bus to the beach and enjoyed the ozone in the air, the surf and sand: he held my arms and dragged me knee-deep into the waves. A thrilling experience – made me forget my home and parents. Of course, a matinee at the Elphinstone on Mount Road occasionally. At Egmore, I had felt hemmed in, the horizon was restricted – but now this boy was opening my eyes to the wide world. I was not yet eighteen, but I possessed all the craftiness needed to save my skin. When my father demanded to know why I was late, I would always say that I had had a special class or was on an excursion with the teachers or doing joint study with a friend in some difficult subjects. My father, battling all day with carpenters to execute his constantly overdue orders, would not probe further. Fortunately, I was passing my exams and that was what he was particular about. But my mother, who had possessed sounder instincts, took me aside while I was leaving for school and said, 'I can hear your evening school bell quite clearly, remember. If you are not here within ten minutes of the bell, I'll tell your father. You know what he will do if he is upset. He will chip the skin off your back with his tools.'

"The next few days I came home punctually at the end of the school, avoiding the young man's company. When he cycled up and brought us magazines, my mother told him, 'We don't have time for magazines. You may stop.'

"'Why? Why?' he asked. And I could hear my mother's answer, 'That's so, that's all, go . . .'

"He hesitated, 'Perhaps uncle may want to read.'

"'Uncle! He is not your uncle! Begone!' she shouted, while my father kept himself deliberately in the shed, away from the scene. Listening to it all, I felt a sudden pity for the fellow and for all the kindness he had shown me, and I dashed out to say, 'Why should you be so rough?' At which my mother slapped my face and I ran in crying.

"I became a virtual prisoner in the house — allowed only to get to my school and back under strict surveillance, escorted by Thayi, our old servant maid. My mother seemed a terrible woman in those days. I stopped talking to her, answered her questions in monosyllables, and whenever I thought of the boy, my heart bled for him. Leaning on his bicycle bar, he was bewildered by all the rudeness he was encountering in the world. I missed the warmth of his company and his enlightening talk, and above all the timid pecking on the neck and hugs when none was looking.

"Though we were apart, we still found a way to communicate. Little notes or bits of paper passed between us through the agency of the woman chaperoning me. At the circulating library she dropped my note on his desk and brought back an answer. Thus I saved my head from being sawn off. To that extent, I respected, or rather *we* respected my parents' command. My final examination was due in a few months. I was not going to do anything that might disrupt my studies. So I acted the model child at home, and my parents looked very happy and pleased, and plied me with their kindness and trust. I concentrated on my studies and did well in my examinations in March. Although I felt desperate sometimes for his company we kept up our show till the May of that year when the results were announced.

"Occasionally we did meet when my parents were away. My mother's family lived at Avadi, fifty miles away. My father would escort her in the morning and they would come back by the evening train, which would leave me free for a full day. They would always warn: 'Don't leave the house, take care of everything. Take care.' The old servant would be told to stay to guard me from intruders (which was my mother's indirect way of indicating the young man). But I bribed the old lady to guard the house and that left us free to visit the circulating library. This would be our happiest moment. He would lock up his little office and take me out. We would go out to the farthest place possible, most times Elliot's Beach in Adyar, which was another planet as far as Egmore citizens were concerned. Elliot's Beach has one or two shacks where sea-bathers could dress – ideal retreats for lovers. All afternoon we stayed in a shack: they were happy hours.

We were recklessly happy. I took care not to go beyond a certain limit in caresses, cuddling and fondling – though within that limit, we attained supreme happiness. We discussed plans for our future – many alternatives. We stayed in the shack watching fishermen go out to sea on their *catamarans*. Sometimes they would peep into the shack, smile and leave us alone. Sometimes they would demand a rupee or so for cigarettes – and then leave us alone. Thus the hours passed – while we stayed in the pleasure of each other's company – listening to the waves splashing on the shore, blue sea and blue sky and birds diving in and the breeze. All of it made him say: 'Let us go on and on here, why should we go back? Let us stay here till we die.'

"But we had to scramble to our feet when the six o'clock chimes were heard from the San Thome cathedral. My father's train was due at seven at the Egmore Station and he would be home in fifteen minutes walking down the railway track. The old lady showed me the utmost sympathy and cooperation, seemed to get a vicarious thrill out of my romance. If my father threw a searching look around and asked the old woman: 'Is everything all right?' she would answer, 'Yes, of course, the child went on reading the whole day. Oh! how much she reads!'

"'Book? What book?' my father would ask suspiciously, on the alert to find out if it was from the circulating library.

"'I want to prepare for a correspondence course in accounting and borrowed a book from Shanta,' I said.

"He was relieved and happy and commended my studious habits, but also warned me against overdoing it, 'because you have just worked hard for your Matriculation Exam.'

"This kind of deceitful existence did not suit us. I felt rather dirty and polluted. When the results came and I was successful, I made up my mind. The next time my parents left for Avadi, my lover brought an old car, borrowed from one of his well-wishers, to the carpentry shop and took me away. He gave the old woman, my chaperone, ten rupees, and before we drove away told her: 'You must bless us.' I bundled up a change of clothes, while the old woman shed tears at the parting. In a voice shaking with emotion, she placed her hands on my shoulder and said, 'May God bless you with many children!' the only blessed state that she could ever imagine.

"He stopped at a flowerseller's on the way, bought two garlands of jasmine and chrysanthemum, and drove straight without a word to a temple on the outskirts of the city: he seemed to have been busy earlier preparing for our wedding. A priest had lit oil lamps all around the image of some god. He presided over the exchange of garlands, asked us to prostrate before the god, lit a heap of camphor, got a couple of his friends to witness, in addition to God, distributed fruits to the gathering, lit a little flame which we circled, and sounded a bell. He then gave the bridegroom a yellow thread, and told him to tie it round my neck, charged us fifty rupees for his service, issued a rubber-stamped receipt, and we were man and wife."

\*     \*     \*

The lady's volubility overwhelmed me. I felt like the wedding guest whom the Ancient Mariner held in a spell of narrative, preventing his entry into the reception whence the noise of festivities was coming. He wailed that it was late and he should go in, but the Ancient Mariner held him with his eyes, ignoring his appeal and just said, "With my cross-bow I shot the Albatross" and continued his hypnotic narration while the wedding guest beat his chest. I didn't go so far, but went on punctuating her speech with "I think it's time for me . . . college socials to attend and report . . ."

She brushed off my protestations and hints and continued her narration as if only her tongue functioned, not her ears. She was quite carried away by her memories.

"We found an outhouse, a cosy one with a kitchen and bed-sitting room in Poonamalle High Road, and lived there happily, as happily as we could. Both of us worked. He continued in his library, which was now bigger, and he held a senior position with a lot of responsibilities. I was a receptionist at a travel agency. Both of us left at nine every day after breakfast and with a one-item simple lunch to pack and carry. I got up at five a.m. and cooked the food for the day. We returned at different times in the late evening and most days, being too tired to do anything else, ate some cold left-overs and went to bed.

"Occasionally I visited the carpentry to see my parents who had become friendly, perhaps taking a realistic view that they had acquired a son-in-law without spending money on dowry, feasts or celebrations."

When she found me fidgeting and trying to get up, she waved me back to my chair and said,

"Spare me some more time please, I'll finish as briefly as I can, though it's a long story. We may not meet again. While I can hold you, I'm anxious you should know the full story – I've not given up hopes you'll see him again, and you must have the full picture of your hero."

"Oh no, not my hero and I'll not," I protested.

"Please don't interrupt," commanded the Ancient Mariner. "If you don't keep interrupting, I'll finish my story quickly . . . otherwise you may make me forget and I've to go back and forth. Already, I think I missed an important episode. It's a vital link. Have I told you what happened on the day of my wedding and my father found me missing when he came home from Avadi?

"When he found me missing, the man seems to have lost his head completely. The old woman Thayi defended herself by explaining, 'A car came into our gate suddenly: Roja (my name at home) was standing at the door, two young men seized and pulled her into the car and drove away . . . I don't know anything more . . . . I ran down crying but the car was gone.' After that my father went to the Egmore Police Station and gave a written complaint that I was missing and that he suspected kidnapping. Inspector Natesh was a family friend. Many were the table legs and rickety stools that my father had mended for him. He seems to have said with gusto:

"Leave this to me. I'll recover your lost daughter. These are days when young persons try to imitate the cinema stories.'

"He spread his net wide and surprised us at a remote place called Fisherman's Hut, beyond Adyar, where we were hiding but living a beautiful existence. Two policemen came in a jeep with Inspector Natesh. We were just enjoying our lunch on the sea-shore, trying to live all the romantic poetry one has read in one's life. It was awkward when Natesh seized my husband's wrist and put the fetters on. However, he said to me, 'Don't cry – you are all right.'

"We drove back – a long, silent drive back to the city. First halt at the penitentiary, where the young man was dropped and handed over to a sergeant at the office, and then I was taken home and handed over to my parents – the worst kind of homecoming for anyone.

"The young man was charged with abducting and kidnapping a minor under eighteen years of age. A lawyer who was a customer of the circulating library and known to my husband came into the picture at this stage and said: 'This is nonsense. I'll get the young fellow out, first on bail.' Three days later the young man went back to his library as if nothing had happened. After that the case came up, off and on at the Presidency Magistrate's court, adjourned again and again. I went through hell, and so did my husband. The validity of our marriage was questioned, and I had to bear the hostility of my mother and relatives. I felt outlawed and miserable. In addition to all this misery, my father's lawyer coerced me to sign a document to say that I had been abducted and forced into a marriage. Said the legal luminary, 'She is a minor and it cannot be a valid marriage.' They bullied and browbeat me to sign a document charging him with abduction.

"This was the most painful part of the whole drama and I could never forgive myself for doing it. Signing a long story based on the old lady's report. How I had been snatched up from our house when I stepped out to get a couple of bananas from the shop across the street. How suddenly a car pulled up, the door opened and I was bodily dragged into the back seat, and the car sped away. The rest of the story was that I was first taken somewhere and kept a prisoner, locked up and watched, and also tortured until I agreed to go through the exchange of garlands at the temple. My parents and their lawyer stood over me to sign the document, the old woman was asked to put her thumb impression as a witness to the kidnapping part of the story. At first I threw away the pen and wept and went without food, but my parents were firm. They kept saying: 'No girl will be safe in this country unless we act. Young scamps like him must be taught a lesson.' All my pleading was to no avail. Finally they broke my spirit, but assured me: 'Nothing will happen to that scamp. Our lawyer will recommend clemency. All this is just to give him a fright, that's all.'

"'Why?' I asked, 'What has he done? He is my husband.'

"'Husband! Husband!' they laughed, 'Don't keep saying it. You'll be ruining your future! Some rascal – don't mention it outside.'

"Then the lawyer added, 'That sort of marriage is not valid my dear child . . . you are under eighteen.'

"At every session of the hearing, the boy had to stand in the box and face the cross-examination. Being on bail, he could go back to his room or to work after attending court. His lawyer was, however, determined to save him. He got busy investigating and going into old records, located the Government Maternity Hospital where I was born and took extracts from the old registers to prove the hour and date of my birth. He proved that we were married at 3.30 in the afternoon of 18 May 1978, and my birth date and hour according to the hospital register was 11.30 a.m. and so it confirmed that at the time of my marriage I was eighteen years and three hours old, I had become a major with full power to decide my own course of life, and at the time of the so-called abduction, I was thirty minutes past eighteen years. Our lawyer demolished the prosecution's time scheme in a series of cross-examinations. I don't want to go into those details now as I may take time. To be brief, the court declared us properly married husband and wife.

"After the case I joined my husband and we established our home as I have already explained. In the course of time, forgotten were the police case and all the earlier bitterness and the feud. My parents once again doted on me. But the son-in-law could not accept the compromise. He refused to visit them or meet them — one point on which he would never yield, although he never interfered with my visiting my parents. He not only refused to visit them, but kept aloof and silent when they happened to come to see us at Poonamalle Road, always bringing some food or delicacy — but he never touched it in spite of my pleadings. I noticed a new development in him – he had become rather firm and hardened in his outlook. He brooded a great deal and seemed to have undergone a change of personality. It was not the trial and prosecution but my sworn statement read out at court that seemed to have shattered his faith. I could never forget the expression in his face when the lawyer read it out and I had to confirm it in public. Our wedded life had now acquired the dull routine of a fifty-year-old couple. I put it down to physical fatigue on his part, and did my best to cheer him and draw him out, but only with partial success."

I kept murmuring that I had to attend a function, but the Delhi woman continued. I almost expected her to say, "With my cross-bow I shot the albatross." Instead of that she simply said, "He didn't come home one evening – that was the end." Her voice shook a little, and again she fumbled in her handbag for the tiny handkerchief. It was not a moment when I could leave. She could not stop her narration. Even if I left she would still be talking to the stars, which had come out, with the pale lantern of the railway station throwing an eerie illumination around. The goods train had arrived and lumbered along, but still she went on.

At some point when she paused for breath I resolutely got up murmuring, "I'll have to go to a wedding reception, having missed the college socials." She concluded, "A man from our travel agency noticed him at the airport at the Kuwait Air counter. Through our associates at Kuwait I tried to get information about him, but they could not trace him. God only knows what he calls himself now. I seem to have lost him forever."

★　　★　　★

The lady left the next day for Delhi. The station master became maudlin at the parting – a man who was used to seeing off hundreds of passengers each day in either direction, in a cold businesslike manner, had tears in his eyes when the engine pulled up.

"Great woman! She was welcome to stay any length of time – even if the inspector came, I'd have managed without disturbing her."

His wife and children were there to bid her farewell. First time I noticed what a lot of children he had produced under his little roof. I suspected that the Delhi woman must have distributed liberally gifts and tips – not overlooking Muni.

When the engine whistled the lady took out of her handbag her card, and gave it to me remarking,

"Most important – I almost forgot it in this *mela* of leave-taking – although I suspect the masterji held up the train for full ten minutes."

I accepted her card and promised, "If I get the slightest clue I'll reach you by every means of communication possible."

★　　★　　★

I found Rann moping and felt sorry for his lonely alienated existence. I declared with extra cheer, "Time to be up and celebrate."

"What?" he asked without much enthusiasm, thinking that it was a bit of a joke.

I said, "The lady has left for Delhi by the 7 Up."

"Are you serious?" he asked.

72

"Absolutely. Just an hour ago. My hands are still warm with all the handshakes. We all broke down at the parting."

"Oh, where, where is she gone?"

"I've told you, Delhi. Not to the next station – far-off Delhi."

He nearly jumped out of the easy-chair. I said, "Let us go out for a walk after a visit to The Boardless."

"Where?" he asked without moving.

"To the river."

"You have it at your backyard."

"This is no good now; much better at Nallappa's Grove, beyond Ellamman Street."

He hesitated at first. I talked him out of his reluctance. Finally he agreed. "How should I dress?" he asked.

"Better tie a *dhoti* around your waist and wear a half-sleeve shirt."

He had bought these recently at the Khadi Stores, made in handspun material.

"If you wear Khadi, they'll respect you, take you for a nationalist, a follower of Mahatma Gandhi."

"He was a great man," he exclaimed irrelevantly.

"That's all right. Get ready, let us go."

"I'm not used to a *dhoti*. I can't walk. It keeps slipping down to my ankles, can't make it stay around the waist."

"All right, come in any dress you like ... I'll wait outside."

I sat on the *pyol* and waited for him. He had the sense to appear in a shirt and grey trousers, but still, when we went down Market Road, people looked

73

at me, as if questioning, "What is this oddity always keeping you company?"

"I feel uneasy when they stare at me."

"No harm, better get used to it. I don't know what it is like in Timbuctoo, but here we don't mind staring, actually encourage it. It gives people a lot of pleasure. Why not let them please themselves that way? It costs nothing."

He wouldn't say anything but fixed his gaze on the far-off horizon, looking at no one in particular.

I said, "No one will mind if you stare at them in return. You miss a great deal by not staring. It's a real pleasure and an education, really." He said nothing but took it as a sort of perverse quipping on my part, probably saying to himself, Cranky journalist. We reached Ellamman Street which dissipated into sand, beyond which the river curved away gently. People were sitting around in groups, students, children, old men, ancient colleagues and pensioners, young men hotly arguing, and of course also a peanut vendor going round crying his ware. On the main steps, people were washing clothes and bathing in the river, or reciting their evening prayers sitting cross-legged. I found a secluded spot near Nallappa's Grove where bullock carts and cattle were crossing. I selected a boulder for a seat so that Rann could be perched comfortably, while I sat down on the sand. The hum of Market Road reached us, but softly, over the chatter of birds settling down for the night in the trees. I realised that he was responding to the quality of the hour – the soft evening light with the rays of the setting sun touching the top branches of trees, the relaxed happy atmosphere with children running about and playing in the sand. He said all of a sudden,

"Have you noticed the kinship that seems to exist between sand and children? It's a feature that I have noticed all over the world – in every part of the globe, in any continent."

I was happy to note his sudden eloquence. "It's one of the things that unites mankind and establishes the sameness. Sand and children and this . . ." he said all of a sudden stooping and pulling out a bunch of some tiny obscure vegetation from the ground. A plant that was hardly noticeable under any circumstance . . . a pale tuft of leaves and a stalk with little white flowers. His eyes acquired a new gleam – unseen normally. "This is the future occupant of our planet," he said in a tone of quiet conviction: "This is a weed spreading under various aliases in every part of the earth – known in some places as Congress weed, don't know which congress is meant, Mirza Thorn, Chief's Tuft, Voodoo Bloom, the Blighter and so on. Whatever the name, it's an invader, may have originated out of the dust of some other planet left by a crashing meteor. I see it everywhere; it's a nearly indestructible pest. Its empire is insidiously growing – I have surveyed its extent and sent a memorandum to headquarters."

I refrained from asking, Which headquarters? Like the word "project" it's a tabloid word which needs no elucidation. He went on as if inspired: "No one has found a weedicide capable of destroying it. They seem to go down at the first spraying, we tried it in Uganda, but a second generation come up immune to it . . . I have calculated through computers that, at the rate of its growth, the entire earth will be covered with it as the sole vegetation by about A.D. 3000. It'll have left no room for any other plant life; and man will starve to death as no other growth will be possible and this has no food value – on the contrary, it is a poison. You will notice that cattle don't touch it. In addition to other disservices, it sucks and evaporates all the ground water. We should call it the demon grass. My notes on this are voluminous – and the book, when it comes, will be a sensation."

"What's your field of study?" I could not help asking. I suspected he was egging me on to do so, why not oblige him? I was feeling kindly toward him. I was softening. His outlandish style of living and dressing was fascinating. Why should I grudge him a little attention, a fellow who was giving me so much entertainment?

He seemed pleased at my query. "Call it futurology – a general term which involves various studies we have to make a proper assessment of all our resources and dangers; human as well as material. All kinds of things will have to go into it. We must get a scientific view and anticipate the conditions and state of life in A.D. 3000. To know whether we shall, as the human species, survive or not."

I could not help bursting into a laugh. "Personally, I wouldn't bother – what, ten centuries hence, none of us, even the most long-lived, will not be involved . . . so . . ."

"How do you know?" he asked. "Present developments in biology and medicine may prolong life endlessly."

"You crave for immortality. I don't care."

"Whether you crave for it or not, that's not the question. We are moving in that direction willy-nilly, and it's important to assess how much of present civilisation is going to survive ... taking into consideration various conditions and symptoms."

"You remind me of our psychology professor who used the words 'tensions', 'symptoms', and 'trends' at least once every nine seconds, when I was a student."

He didn't like my frivolous attitude and suddenly became silent.

★   ★   ★

The reason why I wanted to puncture this pompous fellow was this: the old man at the Town Hall library had a granddaughter who brought him a flask of coffee and some tiffin in a brass container at about three in the afternoon most days. The old man, who came after an early meal to the library before 10 a.m., faded progressively in his chair until the tiffin came, and if any of the readers at the library asked a question at that time, he barked out his reply and looked fierce. "My fate has not decreed me a better life than sitting here guarding dusty volumes. Don't add to my troubles. If you don't see the book, it's not there, that's all. . . . Go, go take your seat; don't stand here and block the air, please." This would be his mood on the days when the girl came late, but generally she was punctual. At the sight of her, his face would relax. He would welcome her with a broad smile, and say, "Baby, come, come! What have you brought me today?" The sight of her brought him endless joy. He would get up from the chair and say: "You sit here, child – I'll come back." He carried the little plastic handbag with the flask and tiffin packet to a back room, beyond which was a washroom with a tap. While he was gone the girl occupied his seat, and listened to the water running in the washroom and then stopping and, after an interval, running a second time, and she would know that he washed his hands before touching the tiffin and washed again after eating, and she would get up and vacate the seat for him as he returned, timing it all perfectly. As expected by her, he would reappear wiping his lips with a checked towel and beaming with contentment.

"Was it all right?"

"Yes, of course, can't be otherwise . . ."

"Grandmother got sugar from the neighbour. We had run out."

"Tell her, I'll buy some this evening on my way home."

The girl was about seventeen years old. He called her "baby" and derived a special joy in thinking of her, watching her come and go, and talking to her. She was at Albert Mission in the BA class. Tall, and though not a beauty, radiated the charm of her years.

Rann came into the library one afternoon when the girl was occupying the chair. Just then I was rummaging in the old newspaper sheets on the central table, searching for some information, what it was I forget now. I was at the newspaper end of the hall and he didn't notice me, but I could see him as he approached the table and halted his steps, with all his faculties alert and tense like a feline coming upon its unsuspecting prey.

Ah! he seemed to say, I didn't know that the Town Hall library possessed this treasure! Is that old fellow gone and my good fortune has put you in his place? He greeted the girl with an effusive, ceremonious bow, and put on an act of the most winsome manner. I wanted to cry out, Keep away, you – I don't know what to call you! She is young enough to be your daughter. You are a lecherous demon and wouldn't mind even if it were a granddaughter! Keep off!

The girl said something and both of them laughed. I wished the old man would come back from his lunch, back to his seat. But he was in the habit of reclining on an easy-chair and shutting his eyes for fifteen minutes. It was generally a calm hour at the library and he left the girl to take care of things for a while, which seemed to be a god-sent chance for Rann. I felt it was time to apply the brake. I folded the newspaper, put it away, got up, and approached the table. The girl cried from the table,

"Uncle, here is an interesting gentleman from Timbuctoo. I didn't know there was such a place! Where is it?"

"Ask him," I said, not ready to be involved in a geographical problem.

Rann rose to the occasion. He took a few steps to the table and demanded, "Get a piece of paper, I'll show you." On the blank sheet, with a stylish slim gold pen, he drew a map. When he said, "You see this is where we are. Timbuctoo is –" the girl brought her face close to his. I'm sure he was casting a spell at that moment, for it seemed to me that the girl was relishing the smell of the after-shave lotion and hair-cream, which, I suspected, made him irresistible to women. He knew it and turned it on fully. With his palm resting on the map, he manoeuvred and agitated his forefinger and middle finger as if playing on a musical instrument, to indicate places, volubly explaining historical, topographical, economic matters of Timbuctoo in detail; he looked up from time to time to ask, in a sort of intimate whisper, Now do you understand? I feared that he was going too far, rather too close to her, when the old man reappeared with the plastic bag in hand, the very picture of contentment, and threw a kindly look at the visitor. He was not overwhelmed by the other's personality as on the first day since Rann was no longer in a three-piece suit but had adapted himself to a normal Malgudi executive costume — cotton pants and shirt-sleeves. The girl rose to give up her seat to her grandfather, who lowered himself in the chair saying, "Long time since we met, how have you been, sir?"

"Thanks," Rann said with a bow. I noted how accomplished an act he was putting on. He was versatile: — one moment to impress the girl and patronise her and take her under his wing — so solicitous, kindly in tone — the world of the fairy-tales, the next moment the international scholar academician adopting his manner to impress the old man — on whose goodwill he would have to depend in order to get closer to the girl.

And there were other reports I was getting about Rann from here and there that I did not like at all.

At The Boardless, Gundu Rao, a horticulturist (in municipal service and responsible for maintaining the nominal park around the Town Hall, the struggling lawns at the Central Police Station and the Collector's Office, and for seeing that the fountain sprayed up and rose to the occasion on national festivities such as Gandhiji's birthday and Independence Day), approached my table to whisper: "Want to tell you something . . ."

Varma who was watching us said: "What secret?"

Rao simpered and replied, "Nothing important."

Varma having to listen to so much all day left us alone. When I had finished the coffee, I found the horticulturist waiting in the street, leaning on his bicycle. He said,

"That man in your house. Who's he?"

"Why?" I asked, resenting his method of enquiry.

"You see . . . you know the Protestant Cemetery far out on Mempi Road?"

"Yes, though I have had nothing to do with it."

"I have been asked to trim the hedges and some of the border plants. The Collector called me and told me to take it up – I don't know why this interest in the cemetery, not my business, really, but I must obey orders."

"Naturally, but you were trying to say something else?"

"Ah, yes, about that man who is living with you. I notice him often there, sitting on a far-off bench in a corner - always with a girl at his side. I know who she is, but I won't tell you. That place is at least five miles out – it's my fate to cycle that distance everyday – such a strain really – but if I don't go the old gardener who lives in a shed won't do a thing and the Collector will come down on us, though I can't understand what the Collector has to do with the cemetery!"

"All right, tell me more about that man."

"Well, I wondered why they had come so far and how; but then I noticed a scooter parked at the gate – and he rides down with the girl sitting at his back – as they do nowadays. Not my business really, when a man and a woman sit close to each other, I generally stay away – it makes me uncomfortable –"

And then Nataraj, manager of the Royal Theatre, met me at the magistrates' court verandah and said,

"You don't come to my theatre at all, why? I have improved the seating and upholstered the sofas, with foam rubber cushions and nylon covers – why don't you drop in some time and write a few words about our improvements? We are showing a picture with a karate expert acting in it. Full house, every show, I tell you. Your guest reserved two sofas in the balcony a couple of days ago. He appreciated the new designs and furnishing – coming from one who has seen the world –"

And Jayaraj, the photographer at the Market Arch, who is really the main reservoir of local gossip (with several tributaries pouring in about people and their doings), where I generally stop to know what's happening everywhere, said,

"Your guest is very active nowadays. He used to hire a cycle from Kennedy, but that poor fellow has lost the regular customer. You know why? Because

Sambu seems to have surrendered his Vespa scooter to him freely. You know why the scooter for the gentleman?"

"Because he has a pillion rider?"

"You know who it is?"

"Yes, yes, I guess."

"And so that's that! He is very attentive to the girl," he added with a leer. He was in his element with gossip of this stature in hand. "You know what his routine is? At 10.30 he is ready behind the Town Hall compound, as 10.35 the girl materialises on the pillion of Sambu's Vespa, 10.45 Kismet Ice-Cream Stall at New Extension, 10.58 at the level-crossing so that she may walk up to the Albert Mission College gate as if she had come walking all the way. After the college she is met again at the level-crossing – and where they go after that is their business, don't ask me."

Others also mentioned the subject – each in his own way. The old man at the library, during one of my morning visits, said, "I see very little of Baby nowadays. She used to bring my tiffin, but I walk home for my tiffin nowadays, leaving the watch to some known person in the reading room. Obliging fellows really – some of the old library users. I even take a few minutes' nap after tiffin and come back. But Baby never comes home before eight nowadays – final year for her and special classes and joint studies every day, I suppose. Nice to think she will be a graduate soon. Then what? Up to her parents to decide. But you know my son-in-law is not a clear-headed fellow – too much of a rustic and farmer and his wife, my daughter, has developed almost like her husband although I had visions of marrying her to a city man in Madras or Calcutta, but this fellow was rich and was studying at Madras and I thought he would pass a civil service exam, but the fellow settled in their village when his father passed away – and now his mind is full of cowdung and its disposal, and a gobar gas plant which utilises it. He and his wife can talk of nothing else – but gas, gas, gas, which lights their stoves and lights everything. Baby, when she goes to her parents for a holiday, cannot stand that life though I insist upon her spending at least ten days with her parents – I brought her away when she was ten so that she could have her education. After she finishes her college, what? That's the question that bothers me day and night. I'd like her to become an officer somewhere – but not too far away. Also I want her to marry and be happy – and again stay not too far away from me. I'm so accustomed to her presence – my wife too says we should not live too far away from her. Anyway let us see what God proposes."

At this point an old reader approached us to ask, "The tenth page of the *Mail* is missing."

"What's special in it?"

"Crosswords," the man said.

The old man replied, "I suspected so." He took it out of his drawer and gave it with the warning, "Copy it down, don't mark on the paper."

★   ★   ★

I bottled up my uneasiness at these reports. I had no clear notion what I could do about the situation or why. It was not my business, I said to myself, but then I began to have suspicions about Rann's background. Before tackling him, I wanted to arm myself with facts. I had no other recourse but to act as a spy. These days he went out after breakfast and kept away till lunch, came in and went out again. I realised that his movements were based on Girija's timetable. When he left in the afternoon I could count on his absence all evening till eight o'clock or longer. I opened his room with a duplicate key. When I stepped in I felt like a burglar in my own home. I felt excited and hard-pressed for time. I quickly examined his briefcase and a portfolio of letters – quite a handful. Envelopes addressed to different names – only two to Rann – and the address was always Poste Restante in different towns and countries. Like our gods, he seemed to have a thousand names – Ashok, Naren, D'Cruz, John, Adam, Shankar, Sridhar, Singh and Iqbal and what not. The letters were all from women: imploring, appealing, and accusing and attacking in a forthright manner; some of them were intensely passionate from Mary, Rita, Nancy, Manju, Kamala, and so on. One or two had been addressed to Dubai or Kuwait, and forwarded from place to place. And there were some from Roja herself, who somehow managed to reach him. There was a common feature in every letter: the cry of desertion. A few blackmail attempts, some threats to inform the police and set Interpol on his track. You would have needed a world map to mark his movements as deduced from the postmarks and the various postage stamps – quite an album could be made with stamps from his envelopes. No wonder he had so many pursuing him, but unable to get at him. "You are heartless – a monster, don't you have a feeling for the child you pampered, who is crying for you night and day? How can he understand the perfidy of your action in melting into the night without even a farewell kiss?" Another letter said, "Come back, that's enough for me. I'll forget the money." In another, "You need not come – if you appear at my door, I'll throw you out. Only return the share due to me – at least 20,000 pesos and you may go to the devil. If you ignore this, I'll write an anonymous letter to the Interpol." This last made me wonder if he was a drug trafficker too. He had a way of slipping away from address to address: it puzzled me why he left any postal addresses at all, and was not afraid of being discovered while collecting mail. He must have had a pathological desire to collect letters and preserve them. This was rather puzzling. Why would any man treasure such correspondence? – enough to damn him and send him to prison. Extraordinary man! I admired on one side his versatile experience, indifference and hardihood. What was the great driving force in his life? picked up a fat bound book, which seemed to be a journal written from time to time. I was nervous about going through it. If I sat reading it, I might not notice the time passing and he might come back. And so I hurriedly gave it a glance, opening a page here and there. Why this man perpetuated his misdeeds in chronicles was beyond my understanding. On one leaf he noted, "No use hanging on here. S is proving impossible. No woman supposes that a man has any better business than cuddling and love talk." Another entry said, "My project is all important to me. I am prepared to abandon everything and run away if it is interrupted. Again and again I seem to fall into the same trap like a brainless rat. It is difficult at this stage to make others see the importance of my book – which has to go side by side with the project even if it is only an offshoot. The world will be shaken when the book is out. The highest award in the world may not be beyond my dream." He noted on another sheet, "Your Majesty, King Gustav and Queen, Members of the Nobel Committee – I'm receiving this award, I feel you are honouring my country. India and Sweden have much in common culturally." I heard the hall clock chime five, and quickly put all the letters and diary back in their original place in the drawer, shut the drawer, locked it as before and quickly and quietly withdrew, leaving no thumb impression on anything.

★     ★     ★

"What do you think of that girl?" I asked him innocently one day.

"Which girl?" he asked.

"Girija – the librarian's granddaughter, whom he calls Baby."

"I don't know," he said, "I don't know her very well – though I see her here and there – especially at her school whenever I go there to see one of the professors. Now that you ask, she is quite smart, and will go far with proper training. But this place is no good for her. She must get out of this backwood, if you don't mind my saying it."

I was rather irked. "But you seem to prefer this to a lot of other places in the world."

"My job is different – but for a young mind starting in life, a more modern, urban, cultural feedback will help. My private view is, don't quote me, from what I have seen, she shouldn't grow up with her grandfather. A hostel would be preferable – where she can compare and compete with her age-group. Anyway after her final exam in March, she should decide her future."

"Marriage?"

"Oh, no, not necessarily, though I would not rule it out. A girl can be married and still pursue intellectual and social values. But the important thing is she should get out of this –"

"Backwood." I completed his sentence. He only smiled. Impossible to fathom his mind's workings.

★   ★   ★

The old librarian said, "Girija is lucky. That man has agreed to coach her through. He seems to be an expert in certain subjects. What do you think of it?"

I hesitated. It was a complex situation. I did not know how far the old man was aware of the situation. In his zeal to see his granddaughter well placed he might welcome Rann's proposal. I couldn't understand anything until I could speak to Girija, but it had become impossible to get at her, though formerly I always enjoyed a little banter with her at the library. Now I remained silent while the old man waited for my comment. One or two at the reading-room table paused, looked up and turned in our direction expectantly. I said to the old man to put the eavesdroppers off the track, "It's getting unusually warm these days —" and left, at which the inquisitive souls at the long table looked disappointed and resumed their reading.

I returned to the library at closing time with the definite objective of talking to the old man when others would not be there. The old man was closing the windows, pushing the chairs back into position, and giving a final look around before locking the door.

"What brings you here at this hour?" he asked.

"I was passing this way and I thought I might as well stop by. I'll walk with you."

He tucked his old umbrella under his arm, its bamboo handle dark yellow with the age-old contact with his fingers, and strode off. I pushed my bicycle along. He lived nearby — fifteen minutes away — at old Palm Grove, in a small house with its broad cement platforms overlooking the street. All the way down he was talking of Girija and her future, which seemed to be very bright. I dropped the idea of warning him about Rann. I felt I'd be making myself unpopular if I spoke against Rann.

He invited me in. I leaned the bicycle against a lamp post and sat down on the *pyol*. He excused himself and went in for a wash, and came back drying himself with a towel and bade me come in, and settled down in the easy-chair. He had hung up his upper cloth on a nail and the shirt over it, his bare body covered with the towel.

"Only two of us in this house — and Baby, you see that's her room. You may peep in if you like."

To please him, I went in and dutifully peeped. She had a small table on which were heaped her books and papers, and clothes on a little stand, again in a heap. On the wall she had pasted up some portraits of film stars and one or two gods also; on the latter she had stuck flowers. A small window opened on the next house; there was only a small bulb throwing a dim light. "She always studies in the hall, sitting on the floor with her books spread about," complained the old gentleman. "Not a soul in the house to disturb her. When she is reading I tiptoe around, and her grandmother doesn't dare raise her voice. Our only interest is to see her pass with distinction, and she must get a Government of India scholarship too."

Meanwhile his wife who had gone to a neighbour's came back. He introduced me to her as the host of the distinguished foreigner, and added, "He is a Kabir Street man. They are not ordinary men there." He gave a grand account of my ancestors.

The venerable lady added her own knowledge of my family members, traced various relationships, and claimed also kinship with one of my aunts, whom I had never heard of. She said:

"You are really fortunate to have a guest of such distinction. Good guests really bring us honour. There was a time when I used to cook and feed with my own hands any number of men and women, not here but in our original home at Gokulam. Well, we had to move here – that was God's will. My daughter was not married at that time – Girija was born in this house when we lost that house –"

"Why do you tire the gentleman with that old tale?"

None the less she continued: "My husband was the registrar of the District Court –"

"Don't be absurd. I was only a sheristedar, not the registrar. I've corrected you a hundred times."

"What if! You had so much money coming in every day and so many visitors – no one would come bare-handed. We had no need to go to the market for anything: vegetables and fruits or rice –"

"Friendly people all round in those days," he explained.

I understood what this meant: a court sheristedar had favours to dispense in the shape of judgement copies, court-orders and so on, and he favoured court-birds in his own way.

The old man did not feel comfortable and tried to change the topic.

"Only after I retired did I take up the library work – convenient, being close to this house. When I hesitated, the judge who started the reading room, whose portrait is on the wall beside Sir Frederick Lawley's, compelled me to accept it, as a sort of social service. On the opening occasion – it was a grand function – he also referred to me in his speech."

I suspected the judge accepted bribes chanelled through the sheristedar. "I must have been in high school at that time," I added.

The lady said, apropos nothing, "Dr Rann came here a couple of days ago. Girija brought him. He is such a simple man – absolutely without conceit – considering his status. He has held such great posts in so many countries – knows so much! I could have listened to him all night! His conversation is so absorbing, but my husband felt sleepy – I insisted the distinguished visitor have food here, and he enjoyed it, though our fare was simple and we couldn't give him porcelain dishes or a spoon. He ate with his fingers! Only thing, he could not sit on the floor like us."

When I got back home, I saw the light in Rann's room. I had an impulse to go and demand an explanation as to what game he was trying to play, to warn him to keep off, and not to add one more desperate correspondent to his files. But I felt doubts about my own understanding of the situation. I might be misreading the whole scene. After all, he must have seen enough women, and Girija might mean no more to him than a niece of whom he was growing fond and whom he would like to see develop academically so that she might have a worthy career. The old couple seemed to have developed a worshipful attitude to Rann. They might misunderstand if I said anything contrary to their views; it might seem as if I had evil motives or was envious of the girl's good luck. They might turn round and say, None of your business ... we know. And I could not very well reveal Rann's private affairs. If he walked out of my house it might give rise to public talk, and perhaps compromise the girl and cause an innocent family embarrassment and scandal. I might be misreading the whole situation. After all, a child whom I had been seeing for years, since her Albert-Mission-Nursery-School-uniform days, but now too tall for her age, dressed in perfectly starched and pressed cotton saree and looking quite smart — this wouldn't mean that she was an adult woman capable of devious and dubious adventure. She might well still be a child at heart, like most womanly-looking girls. But if so why the Protestant Church rendezvous? That didn't seem so innocent. If he was only helping her studies and general knowledge, it was not necessary to go so far. . . . Lying in bed I kept sifting and analysing and finding justifications and overcoming doubts and suspicions about Girija and Rann, till I fell asleep well past midnight.

★   ★   ★

Our Lotus Club was twenty-five years old, and we decided to celebrate its Silver Jubilee with a grand public lecture at the Town Hall by Dr Rann of the United Nations, on a brand new subject, "Futurology". Rann somehow accepted the proposal when I mentioned it. He said, "Normally I have an aversion to public speaking. I am a writer, not a speaker. However, you have been good to me, and I can't say no to you. I must oblige you." This was on the day following our evening on the river sand when he had expounded to me his theory of the cosmic extinction of all life through the Giant Weed.

The Lotus Club was desperately in need of a show to boost its prestige, but more than prestige, the Lotus Club had sufficient funds to spend on an occasional burst of activity, and a rich man, decades before, had left an endowment and special fund for the Silver Jubilee. The President, who had been rusting, readily agreed. He was proud to have an international personality to deliver the Jubilee Lecture and on a subject that was so mysterious: "futurology". "Everyone knows what astrology, physiology and zoology are, but no one knows about 'futurology'. I am agog to hear this lecture."

He wanted me to print a brochure entitled "Lotus – Twenty-five Years of Public Service" and distribute it in the hall, also several thousand handbills announcing the meeting, and five hundred special n. vitations printed on decorated cards to be mailed to India's president, prime minister, the editors of national newspapers, every VIP of the land. Nothing could appeal to me more than this activity.

At the Truth Printing Works, the printer Nataraj cleared a corner of the press for me. I sat there in the morning writing up the pages of the Jubilee brochure, arranging the invitations and notices; hot from my desk, the matter was passed to the printer. Nataraj had set aside his routine work and devoted all his energy and time to this task. I felt happy and fulfilled, being so active, and was already worried at the back of my mind as to how I would stand the dull days ahead when all this activity should cease.

The president of the Lotus Club was one Mr Ganesh Rao, a pensioner now but at one time a judge of the Supreme Court at Delhi. My day started with a visit to his bungalow at Lawley Extension. A gracious elder of the community who looked like Lloyd George or Einstein with white locks falling on his nape, he was a prized possession of our town – the citizens remarked with awe and gratitude that after decades of distinguished service at Delhi, Kashmir, and even at some international courts, he should have chosen to return to the town of his origin.

★ ★ ★

Gaffur the taxi driver, whose Ambassador always occupied a position of vantage beside the Fountain-Wall on the Market Road – except at train time when it could be seen under the Gul Mohar tree at the railway station – was the man I was desperately searching for before the big meeting. I had to go round town distributing invitations and notices and on various other errands in connection with the meeting. I had so much to do that I felt the need for a transport quicker than my bicycle or Sambu's scooter, if available.

Gaffur was not to be seen. I had to go in search of him here and there. No one was able to guide me. I was pressed for time; the day of the Jubilee was drawing near. As ever, Jayaraj came to my rescue. He said, "He lives in Idgah – one of those houses. I'll find out and leave word on my way home tonight."

Gaffur's Ambassador was at my door the next morning. He left the car at the street corner and came to my room while I was shaving before my ancient mirror. "Madhu, you want me?" he asked, being one of the boyhood associates who called me Madhu instead of TM. My face was still full of soap. I spoke to him looking from the mirror.

"Gaffur! Where have you been all these days? You have become scarce – and I want you so badly for the next week."

"Madhu, your tenant is the one who keeps me

95

busy. I have to be at his call every morning. I don't call for him here, he doesn't want it that way, but he hails me at the fountain almost at the same hour each day at about ten-thirty, and then he leaves me at five o'clock, after I have returned the girl."

"Which girl? Where do you take her?"

"I think they are going to marry – the way they are talking in the backseat and planning, he is taking her to America . . . though it is none of my business, I can't help listening."

"Oh, God!" I cried, involuntarily blowing off the soap on my lips.

"Why do you worry, Madhu? Is it that you want to marry her yourself?"

"Oh, God!" I cried a second time. "I've known her since she was a baby, and she is like a daughter to me."

"So what?" he said. "You must be happy that she found a nice man for a husband. Otherwise you'd have to spend so much money to get her a husband. After all, in your community, unlike ours, girls are free to go out without a veil and talk to men – and so what is wrong?"

"He is old enough to be her grand-uncle."

"I won't agree with you. He is very sweet, looks like a European. . . . Good man, pays down by the meter without a word, a gentleman. If there were more like him, I could buy a Rolls Royce or a Mercedes Benz."

I left it at that. I learnt a great deal from Gaffur that morning. I had also noticed the past two days that Rann was packing up; and had settled with the furniture company to cart their pieces away after the Jubilee meeting. The plot was revealed by Gaffur: after the meeting at the Town Hall he was to pick up Rann's suitcases from my house, meet Rann at the Town Hall, then drive away to Peak House on Mempi Hills the same night, with the girl, who would be waiting some place. From Peak House they would descend on the other side of the mountain to Mempi Town, and then leave by bus to God knows where. I was shocked by the smooth manner in which Rann was manoeuvring to elope with the girl.

Gaffur's report was invaluable. I had to base my future action on it, but I realised I was facing a delicate situation. I had to avoid upsetting anyone on any side. The old librarian must be protected from shock or a stroke, Girija from a public scandal and an eventual desertion in some far-off place and all the frustration and tragedy that befell every woman captivated by Rann's charms. My mind wandered over morbid details as to how far the girl had admitted him; when it was all over, one must somehow take her to Dr Lazarus, the lady doctor at the Government Hospital, to get her examined for a possible abortion, a lesser evil than being burdened with a fatherless child. While the other women in Rann's life were perhaps hardy and sophisticated, capable of withstanding the tragedy, this girl was innocent, her mind in a nascent state, unless already complicated and corrupted by association with Rann. It was not a good sign that she was lying to her simple-minded grandfather. I doubted if she cared for her studies at all nowadays; Rann might have promised any degree she chose from any university on earth. I could well imagine his boastful assur-

97

ance, "Oh, you leave it to me – I'll speak to Turnbull, president of . . . when we get to the United States." His voice rang in my ears with this sort of assurance, and the picture came before me of this girl looking up at him adoringly. I luxuriated in a passing vision of slapping this girl for her stupidity and shutting her up in a room and kicking out Rann, but on the other hand Rann had to be kept in good humour. If he was upset and backed out and vanished, I'd be hounded out of Malgudi by its worthy citizens for being fooled with all that trumpeting about the Town Hall lecture. Sitting in the meditation room after Gaffur left, I brooded and brooded and came to the conclusion not to speak about anything till the meeting was over. I would pretend not to notice Rann's packing up either.

It was an inspiration. I moved out of the meditation room and rummaged in my desk till I picked up the pocket diary in which I remembered placing the address card of the lady from Delhi. At first it eluded my search – all kinds of other cards, addresses and slips of paper fell out from between the leaves. I almost despaired, then gave a final shake and her yellow card fell out – "Commandant Sarasa, Home Guards Women's Auxiliary, Delhi," with her address, telephone, and telex numbers. I hurried to the post office and sent off a telegram.

COME IMMEDIATELY. YOUR HUSBAND FOUND. COME BEFORE HE IS LOST AGAIN. YOUR ONLY FINAL CHANCE TO ROPE HIM. STAY RAILWAY WAITING ROOM. I'VE FIXED IT. TAKE CARE NOT TO BE SEEN IN TOWN. WILL MEET AND EXPLAIN FURTHER PROCEDURE.

The strategy was perfect.

I had to soften the station master again with a five-rupee note, and he promised to entertain the lady royally in the waiting room as before. I expected her to arrive on the eve of the Jubilee meeting at the Town Hall, when Rann would be preoccupied with both his romantic plans and his preparations for the lecture, now of course facilitated by having Gaffur's taxi at his disposal. I was in suspense while I waited for the train from Madras, but it did not bring the lady in. The second train, from Trichy, also disappointed me. No sign of her. However, she arrived late that night by road from Trichy, where she had flown from Delhi. Her car was parked in the station compound. She woke up the station master and got the waiting room opened.

Having been busy the whole day with a hundred things to do before the meeting, I found time to go to the station master's house only at midnight and was relieved to learn that the lady had arrived. I didn't want to spend any more time at the station. I gave him another token of esteem in cash, as well as a sealed envelope addressed to the Commandant to be delivered to her without fail in the morning. I also gave him a VIP invitation card to attend the Lotus Club meeting, which pleased him tremendously.

My letter, which I had composed under great strain, gave the lady precise instruction as to what she should do next.

★   ★   ★

The extraordinary publicity generated by the Lotus Club brought in a big crowd. On the day of the meeting, the Town Hall auditorium was packed. The organisers were plucky enough to have organised a Deputy Minister to preside, which meant that the local officials could not stay away. The police and security arrangements were spectacular. The Deputy Minister was in charge of Town Planning, Cattle Welfare, Child Welfare, Family Planning, Cooperation and Environment, Ecology and other portfolios too numerous even for him to remember. In Delhi he had six different buildings for his offices and files.

The President of the Lotus Club had written a letter to him requesting him to grace the occasion, and he had readily agreed. Being the most ubiquitous minister one could think of, every day the newspapers carried reports of his movements. Malgudi had been rather left out of his official circuits, but now it was coming on the official map, much to the satisfaction of the towns folk.

When the meeting began, the foot-lights came on. The minister was seated at the centre of the stage in a high-back gilded chair; Rann was seated on his right in a not so high and less gilded chair; and three other chairs were occupied by the President of the Lotus (ex-judge of the Supreme Court) and two other factotums. I was given a seat at right angles to this main row as became the press and also because I was really the creator of the entire function. Behind the minister sat his secretary and behind him a uniformed orderly in a high-rise glittering lace-edged turban.

The hall was packed, as I noted from my position of vantage; students, lawyers, businessmen and a motley crowd of men and women, mostly wives of government officials. A lot of noisy children ran around chasing each other. The organisers were kept busy trying to catch and immobilise them, but the little devils were elusive and ran behind and between the chairs. The distinguished men seated on the dais looked away and tried not to notice, but the ex-judge beckoned to an executive and whispered, "Can nothing be done to quieten these children?"

Whereupon the man went up to the women and said, "Please control your children."

A woman retorted haughtily: "Tell their mothers, not me."

"Where are the mothers?" No answer came. The man was helpless and felt foolish and lost. He caught hold of a boy and whispered to him: "They are distributing sweets over there," pointing outside, and the boy turned round and ran out gleefully, followed by all the other children. "Children from the neighbourhood, not ours," explained someone.

The ex-judge rapped on the table with a paperweight, took a gulp of water from the glass, and began, "We are honoured by the presence of the Honourable Minister." He elaborated the minister's role in building up a first-rate nation. This presentation took twenty-five minutes. He devoted two minutes to Rann the main speaker today, about whom he did not have much to say, and hurried on to call upon the Hon'ble Minister to speak. The Minister, a seasoned orator, clutched the microphone expertly, drew it to his lips, and began:

"My respected elders, the noble mothers of the land, and the distinguished brethren here, we have in our midst a distinguished scholar who has come from afar and has dedicated his life to. . . ." He fumbled for the right word and paused for a second to look at a piece of paper. "Futurology," he went on. "You may ask what is futurology. The speaker of this evening is going to tell us about it. I should leave it to him to explain his subject. I'll only confine myself to what Jawaharlal Nehru said once –" He somehow twisted the context of futurism and whatever meaning it might have, to an anecdote centring around Jawaharlal. And then he explained Mahatma Gandhi's philosophy. "In those days," he reminisced, "I was a *batcha*, but serving our motherland in some capacity, however humble, was my only aim in life, inspired by our leaders and encouraged by them. I was always in the presence of Mahatmaji wherever he camped, and of course Jawaharlal was always with him and so were many of our distinguished patriots and leaders. Though I was a *batcha* Mahatmaji and Nehruji encouraged me to be with them, and if I count for anything today, I owe it to their affection and if I have served our motherland in any capacity, it's through their grace." He managed to add a mention of Lord Mountbatten also as one of his gurus, and then he came back to Mahatmaji and explained how two days before his death, Gandhiji had said to him, "My inner voice tells me that my end is near," and how he, the future Deputy Minister, broke down on hearing this and implored him not to say such things, where-upon Gandhiji said, "Yesterday at the prayer meeting at Birla's house: were you present? Didn't you notice a group at the gate? I could infer what they were saying. . . ."

At this point I noticed a couple of old men nodding in their seats, lulled to sleep by the Minister's voice. I looked at our well-groomed Rann in the full regalia of his Oxford blue three-piece suit – he, too, was bored with the Minister's rambling talk. He kept gazing at the typed sheets as if wondering if he would have a chance at all to lecture. The Minister had gone on for an hour without a scrap of written material, sentences spewing out without interruption. Those who were familiar with his speeches would have understood that as a routine he narrated the Mahatma Gandhi episode at the conclusion. But most of the assembly was unaware of this and now despaired whether they were fated to listen to this man until midnight.

From out of the student group was heard a voice saying, "We want to hear the speaker of this evening." Undaunted by this request, accustomed as he was to hecklers in parliament, the Minister retorted cheerfully, "You are right. I'm also anxious to hear our friend on the subject of –" He had to refer again to the piece of paper. "But let me finish what I was saying. You'll find it relevant to the subject today." And he went on to talk about the importance of rural handicrafts. After fifteen minutes, while his hecklers looked resigned to their fate, he sat down. Then he whispered to Rann at his side: "I'd like to read your speech in the papers tomorrow, I'm sure. Now I've another meeting at Bagal, people will be waiting. Have to finish and drive to Trichy airport – must be back in Delhi tonight. So you will excuse me . . ." When he half inclined his head, his aide stood up and took charge of the Minister's garland, bestowed earlier by the ex-judge, and they left abruptly.

Rann came to the microphone after a formal introduction and abruptly began:

"As you are all aware how near disaster we are – "

"No, not yet," said a heckler in the audience. "Not heard the worst yet. Do go on."

Unperturbed, Rann read on, holding up a warning finger all through. "Man was born free and everywhere he is in chains, Rousseau said."

"No, Voltaire," said the heckler.

"One or the other, it doesn't matter. It's time we noticed our chains, invisible though they may be, these chains are going to drag us down to perdition unless we identify them in good time, and those chains and fetters which are imperceptible now will overwhelm –"

"That's all right, we'll call the blacksmith to file them off. Now go on with your story."

From another group a man shouted, "Throw this wag out. He is disturbing the meeting. Don't mind sir, please go on." At this point a scuffle ensued, and the heckler was dragged out of the hall by a couple of strong men. They came back and said generously to Rann: "Please go on sir, don't mind the disturbance; that fellow disturbs any and every meeting."

Rann resumed his reading. He had the theatricality of a Seventh Day Adventist. His voice rose and fell as in a sort of declamation. He hissed and snorted, sighed and screamed according to the theme of the drama he was developing. The theme was the collapse of this planet about A.D. 3000. When he described, holding aloft a specimen, how the tuft of a grass-like vegetation, an obstinate weed, was going to overrun the earth, people watched without response. But then he went on to say: "This looks insignificant, like the genie within a bottle. Take out the cork and you will see the dimension to which it can grow," and described its tough, persistent growth, told about how by A.D. 2500 half the surface of the globe would be covered up.

"It's a cannibal, in certain places along the Amazon it is actually called the Cannibal Herb, which nomenclature was at first mistaken to mean food for the cannibals, but actually means that it fattens itself on other plants. Where it appears no other plant can grow. It swallows every scrap of vegetation near at hand, root, stalk and leaf; it quenches its thirst by sapping up groundwater however deep the water-table may be. I have in my collection a specimen – a wire-like root three hundred feet long when it was pulled out. Under a microscope at the root-terminal were seen sacs to suck up water. Ultimately no water will be left underground, in rivers or in the sea, when billions of such sacs are drawing up water and evaporating them at the surface.

"Scientists, biologists, biochemists are secretly working on formulations that would eliminate this weed. Secretly because they do not want to create a scare. But the weed develops resistance to any chemical or bacteria and in a second generation that particular culture has no effect. Actually any weedicide acts as nutrition for it. Does this not remind us of the demon in our stories whose drop of blood shed on the ground gave rise to a hundred other demons?"

He went on and on thus and then he came to a further menace: "Are you aware that for one citizen there are eight rats in our country, which means that only one-eighth of the food produced is available for legitimate consumption –"

"What is legitimate consumption?" shouted a voice from the back of the hall. "Have rats no right to eat? They also are creatures of this earth like any of us."

The chuckers realised that the interrupter they had thrown out was back in the hall somewhere, though he could not be spotted.

Someone else cried, "Don't mind him, doctor, go on . . . a crackpot has smuggled himself in."

"I'm no crackpot but also a scholar. I'm a PhD –"

The chuckers stood up to locate the speaker. There was a slight disturbance. Some of those in the audience who felt bored edged their way towards the door. Rann stood puzzled. I whispered to him, "Why do you pay attention to these things, go on, go on."

He continued, "There are dozens of such problems facing us today," and then elaborated for the next forty-five minutes all the things that menaced human survival. Ghastly predictions. His voice reached a screaming pitch when he declared, "The rats will destroy our food stock and the weed will devour everything, including the rats, and grow to gigantic heights although rising in our present observation only at the rate of a tenth of a millimetre per decade, but it will ultimately rise to gigantic heights sticking out of our planet skyward, so that an observer from another planet will notice giant weeds covering the surface of the globe like bristles, having used all the water. If the observer peered closer with his infra-red giant telescope, he would find millions and billions of skeletons of humans and animals strewn about providing bone-meal for this monstrous and dreadful vegetation . . ."

At this point a scream was heard, "Ah, what is to happen to our grandchildren?"

"The lady has fainted. Get a doctor someone."

People were crowding round a woman who had fallen down from her chair. They were splashing water on her face and fanning her.

"Give her air, don't crowd."

Someone was saying soothingly, when she revived, "After all, madam, it'll only be in A.D. 3000. Not now."

"What if?" she retorted.

Another woman was saying, "We don't want to perish in this manner – our children must be saved."

At the sound of the word "children" the fainted lady who had just revived let out a wail and screamed again, "Oh, the children! Take them away somewhere to safety." Many other women began to moan in sympathy and tried to rush out of the hall clutching their children, while the children themselves resisted and howled playfully. "Come away, this place is cursed — not safe. Oh, come away." Several men tried to calm the women down, saying, "Be calm, it will happen only one thousand years later, no danger immediately."

"Who are you to say so? What authority have you to say so? It may happen today."

People were on their feet and the assembly was in complete disarray. The ex-judge, who had escorted the Deputy Minister, strayed out and ultimately disappeared. So did the police. Various spirited young men lifted and smashed the folding chairs. People rushed to the exit in confusion.

"Cobra! A cobra is crawling under the chair! Take care!" a mischievous urchin shouted.

"Where? Where?" People hoisted themselves on benches and chairs. The smashed chairs were collected, heaped up outside and set on fire. Someone switched off the hall lights in the pandemonium, though somehow the stage lights were still on. A gang of toughs approached the dais, armed with the legs and remnants of the splintered chairs and shouted, "Down with —"

While Rann continued to sit stupidly watching the show as if gratified with the preview of the cataclysm he forecast, I tugged him up by his collar, crying, "Come out, you fool, before they kill you."

"Why? Why?" he asked. I dragged him out to the back of the stage, pushed open a door, propelled him into the darkness at the rear of the Town Hall, and led him out to an open space.

Two men approached saying, "This way doctor,

your car is there." They hustled him in the dark. Presently I heard the door of a car bang and then move off. That was all, the final glimpse I had of the man called Rann. Never saw him again.

A postcard arrived a few days later from the Commandant: "This is just a thank-you note. My well-wishers brought Rann to the car in which I was waiting. I am sure he is going to be happy hereafter. I won't let him out of sight again. He asks you please to freight his baggage to our address."

* * *

Gaffur had parked his Ambassador on the drive, a little away from the main entrance to the Town Hall, in half darkness, waiting patiently for his distinguished customer. After the hall emptied, the turbulent crowd had left, and the lights were switched off, I started homeward. As I came down the drive I noticed Gaffur's taxi. "What are you doing here?"

"You know – he asked me to wait here, I don't know, a long drive ahead to Peak House – I've all his baggage in the boot. Picked it up at your house this evening on his order."

"You are hoping for your Rolls-Royce still?" I asked suppressing a laugh.

"Why not?" he asked. "At the rate he is giving me business, I think he'll even want me to drive him to Bombay and Delhi –"

"He's already left for Delhi," I said, and then I told him the story. "You can't blame him. After all, he's gone back to his wife, who has a right, holds an authorised certificate for his role as a husband."

"But what about the girl who is waiting?"

"Where?"

"She has packed up and is waiting at the school verandah. They were supposed to go to Peak House and —"

"Let us go and take her home."

The girl came out running and crying, "Ah! The meeting over? How I wished I were there to listen to you and watch your triumph in public —" She blurted out: "Oh, darling, how happy you must be . . . now we are free —" and checked herself.

Gaffur hurriedly got down from the car and ran to meet her half way to explain the changed situation. When she saw me, she broke down hysterically. "I don't believe you people. You are all against him. He was so good, oh, he was kind and generous and loving. You don't understand him, nobody understands him. Take me to him, wherever he may be, let me know the truth from his own lips. Please, please, I beg you." She went on ranting and lamenting.

I realised that she had a totally different picture of Rann. She worshipped him as a god who could do no wrong. Her face was disfigured with tears and her words, mostly panegyrics of her god, gushed forth in a torrent. I was shocked, never having thought their relationship had grown so deep. I was appalled at the extent to which the affair had grown, and couldn't help picturing it as a spread of the weed Rann was bothered about. No use talking to her about Rann — it would make no impression on her, would not pass through the barrier she had built against the outside world.

We let her go on. Gaffur being my friend, did

not mind wasting time with us. He too had known her since childhood and was bewildered by the transformation he saw. It took us time to persuade her to come to the car. Gaffur carried her trunk. She was so dead exhausted that with a little push we got her into the car and with a further push leaned her back against the seat cushions. She was apathetic and did not care where we went. When we took the turn into Palm Grove Street, she just said, "Don't wake up my grandfather. I'll find my way in."

I hesitated for a moment – it was midnight – but it would have been futile to argue with her. We put her down noiselessly in front of her door with her trunk and sped away with the least noise. We had nothing to say to each other and remained silent till we came to Kabir Street. Stopping at my house, Gaffur said gruffly (he was choking with emotion and was unusually shaken), "What shall I do with his baggage?"

"I'll keep it and send it on later."

"Who pays the meter charge?"

"I'll fix it with the Lotus Club tomorrow."

He drove off gloomily, remarking, "She used to be such a sweet creature!"

★   ★   ★

I found no time to visit the Town Hall library for a week. When I resumed my news-hunting and reporting, I dropped in at the library quietly one morning, and the old man said, "Oh, you. I wanted to see you badly. Where have you been? Do you know Baby has not been well? That outing with her classmates seems to have upset her somehow, eating all sorts of things ... young people ... she came back sooner than I expected. I called Dr Krishna and he has given her some medicine."

"Oh, she'll be all right," I said with a forced cheer.

"We must fulfil our vow at our family temple in the village, and then she will be all right. There has been a lapse on our part," he said.

"Quite, surely, go ahead," I said, suppressing the advice. "Also propitiate Dr Lazarus, that will also help."

★    ★    ★

I rather missed him. Without Rann the front room seemed barren. I felt lonely and bored. I kept the room vacant, hoping for another Rann to turn up, or, who could say, Rann himself might return to complete his masterpiece, or to resume the mission of minding the librarian's granddaughter's higher education. Even that question, though it had upset me at first, didn't seem quite so objectionable now. I had perhaps misread the situation. Their relationship might have been purely platonic. I laughed to myself at this (im)possibility. For platonic purposes one did not have to take a trip to Peak House in Gaffur's taxi. Platonic love did not call for secret, long journeys! Let me not gloss over it, I said to myself. Let me speak the truth unto myself. He was a callous and indiscriminate lecher, and thank God he did not try to lodge her in his room in my house! That would have provoked a riot in Kabir Street, and God knows to what extremes our people might have gone if anything had happened there.

Luckily, nothing came of it – the girl seemed to come through her escapade unscathed. She resumed her studies and attended college regularly; this I verified from time to time through discreet enquiries at the Town Hall library. The old man was always happy to talk of his granddaughter. "Oh, she is too studious nowadays. After her school hours, she just comes home, and writes and reads all evening. Her grandmother is rather worried about her, and wants her to go out and relax with her friends. But she seems to have lost interest in her friends and has become very serious-minded."

In my narrative about Rann at The Boardless, I gave a modified version of the story and generally slurred over all the incidents connected with the girl, to save her from gossip. If anyone questioned me concerning the floating rumours about Rann and Girija, I dismissed their curiosity with contempt as being morbid. But no amount of hedging could keep Rann's abrupt exit from being discussed.

Varma was the first to question me. "So the lady abducted her own husband from the meeting! Wonderful! What happened after that?"

"I may say that they lived happily ever after, from a letter just received yesterday from Commandant Sarasa. She is keeping him in check. I don't think he will try to get away again. After all, husband and wife quarrel, but it can't last: a sound couple will always get over that phase."

Varma was impressed with the wife's determined pursuit and capture of her husband.

"It reminds one of Savitri and Satyavan of our legends. How Savitri persistently followed Yama, the God of Death, when he plucked away her husband's life; how she dogged his steps as he tried to move off, pleading and pleading until he yielded, and how Satyavan, whose body had lain inert in the forest, revived and joined his wife. I think this Commandant is a similar one."

I left him and his cronies to draw whatever conclusion they pleased, without contradicting anyone. I suspected that somewhere in his thirty-year collection of calendars Varma surely had a sheet in colour litho of Savitri pestering Yama; most of his philosophical conclusions were derived from such representations on his walls.

The fiasco at the Town Hall was a passing sensation as far as The Boardless community was concerned; the confusion was a result of some thugs who had got into the hall only to disturb and break chairs. But one of the members explained:

"It seems the lecturer threatened to blow up the earth with an atom bomb. I was not there, of course, but my nephew, who is studying at Albert Mission, told me that the lecturer made a threatening speech."

His listeners murmured an approval of the manner in which the function ended.

"But the Deputy Minister's speech was wholesome and inspiring, I learn," added someone else.

I never corrected any statement or defended Rann. Not my business.

★　　★　　★

But I constantly speculated on Rann's present plight – the tethered domesticity, which he must be facing in far-off Delhi. I was hoping to hear from him, but he never wrote, probably resenting the manner in which he had ended his lecture and fallen into a trap.

Six months later one evening while posting a letter in the mail van of 7 Down, the station master came excitedly to announce, "The lady is in the waiting room – arrived in a jeep this afternoon!" I looked and there she stood, filling up the threshold of the waiting room in her khaki uniform, an over-whelming presence. She waved to me and turned in, opened the door a few minutes later and came out in civilian dress – a pale yellow saree. She looked enormously powerful as she greeted me with a laugh: "You never expected to see me, but I am here now." She had two chairs put out under the tree as before, looked at the station master hovering around to do her bidding. She told him,

"Masterji – I hope the timetable is unchanged, and we won't be disturbed till the goods train arrives at eleven."

"Yes madam, how well you remember!"

"Tell your good wife, I shall need nothing more than a banana and a glass of milk – advised to avoid all food at all times! I shall call for my milk and fruit by and by – till then please leave us alone, we have to talk over important matters." Turning to me, she said, "TM, no excuses today. You will have to sit through and listen to me fully. I'm pressed for time. I've been sent south for a survey of rural areas – last two days I was busy travelling around in a jeep. Painful business, jeep travel. I'm pressed for time, leaving for Trichy airport at five in the morning and then on to Delhi by noon. Have to tell you a lot. Sit down and stay down. If you feel hungry, I'll ask the master to give you something to eat. But don't go. You have to listen to me."

Without coming to the point she was talking in general terms, since she suspected that the station master and Muni must still be around, ready to listen to our talks. When she was sure they were gone, she leaned forward and whispered, her voice quivering, "Your friend has vanished again!"

I had sensed that some such statement was coming and said involuntarily, "I thought so."

She begged, "If he is here, please give him up again – I agreed to this trip in the hope that he might be here again, although I knew it was a hopeless hope."

"I wish with all my heart I could help you again. But believe me, he is not here. I have no information. I've not heard from him at all."

I repeated it several times to emphasise that I was speaking the truth. She fished out of her handbag a tiny kerchief, touched her eyes, blew her nose and said, "These few months have been our happiest ones. It seemed a revival of our far-off days in Madras – he managed to convey the same charm and warmth. But for our physical changes and age, which the outside world might notice. As far as we were concerned, we were back in the days of my father's carpentry, on the bench under the tree, whispering to each other. Such revived moments made one forget the present conditions. The joy in each other's company and the sense of fulfilment were complete and indescribable. At such moments I thought of you with profound gratitude. But alas, I could not give him enough time. I left home for the Parade

Ground at six in the morning, returned home off and on, being mostly out on various official duties. Sometimes I had to be away for a couple of days or more touring the countryside. Heavy work, I liked it. He appreciated my work and was full of praise and encouragement, and looked after himself and the home. Such a domesticated creature one could not imagine. He lived a very well regulated life – sought no society-life or diversion, being completely absorbed in his writing and studies. He mentioned that his work was progressing smoothly at a faster rate than at any time in his life, and regretted that he should have missed this wonderful life with me. We found time to sit and talk only late in the evening after I had shed my official uniform and changed into a saree. We had chairs put out in the garden and sat there till late at night, even carrying our supper out under the stars. At about eleven he would return to his study and shut himself in, worked, I suppose far into the night. He often said that his book, when it came out, would shake all our ideas to the foundation. He jogged in the morning in the park nearby, went for a stroll in the evening through shopping crowds at the market, and demanded nothing more nor sought any other company. I left him absolutely alone, respected his desire for privacy. When I noticed letters coming to him from different countries, I feared he might be in touch with his old friends, but I suppressed that suspicion as unworthy – he was a man to be loved, respected and above all trusted."

She laughed now bitterly. "All wrong ideas and misleading notions. I tell you he had unsuspected depths of duplicity. At the initial stages I did not trust him so fully and had his movements watched, but I gave that up in due course, for it seemed unnecessary and mean. Thus we passed our time. It was pleasant but I was also feeling apprehensive without any reason, only because it seemed too good to last. And it actually turned out so.

"Ten days ago I had to be away in Jaipur for three days on special duty. I couldn't take leave of him – he hadn't opened his door yet. It was my usual practice to leave without disturbing him. When I returned home, three days later, it was all over, the old story again. The cook told me that he had gone soon after breakfast the day I left, taking a suitcase and a trunk with him. A car came for him with a woman in it. I wondered who she might be and where she came from, and how he could have arranged all this. He had left a letter on the hall table for me."

She held out the letter for me to read. It just said: "Good-bye dearest. I have to be off again. It was lovely while it lasted – thanks!"

"What do you make of it?" she asked.

"He must have received a sudden call connected with his research, I think."

She laughed bitterly. "But who is the woman?"

"Perhaps a research assistant?"

"No, a nurse from Matilda's. I checked everywhere for missing persons, and one Komal at Matilda's had vanished suddenly, resigning her job. Don't ask me how he could have organised it all, or how he managed to cultivate the nurse or how long it must have gone on. He was an expert in the art of deception. Now I realise that all along he must have lived a parallel secret life while creating the impression of living with me. I visited various airlines and the airport, and got the information that he had taken a flight to Rome on the same day I left for Jaipur. From Rome he could radiate on to any continent with his latest companion! I can only conclude from the description I got at one of the airline counters that the passenger was your Rann of Malgudi, a special name he seems to have conjured up for your edification. God alone knows under how many names he goes about and how many passports he has manufactured. An expert, really, in his own field. I pray to God that some day he may be caught at least for his passport frauds and made to spend the rest of his life in some hellish prison. I've no hope of seeing him again."

At this point she broke down, and began to sob uncontrollably. Between her fits of sobbing she managed to say, "I should have been far happier if I had never met you or noticed your news item about the Timbuctoo man. Or it would have been best if I'd listened to my father's advice to keep away from him."

It was distressing to see a mighty personality, generally self-possessed, crumbling down. My eyes were wet too. Presently finding it embarrassing to continue in my presence, she abruptly got up, rushed back to the waiting room, and bolted the door.

# Postscript

I had planned *Talkative Man* as a full-length novel, and grandly titled it, "Novel No. 14". While it progressed satisfactorily enough, it would not grow beyond 116 typewritten sheets, where it just came to a halt, like a motor car run out of petrol. Talkative Man, the narrator, had nothing more to say. He seemed to feel, What more do you expect? This is only the story of a wife's attempt to reclaim her erratic, elusive husband who is a wanderer, a philanderer on a global scale, abandoning women right and left. I have told you his story as far as I could confine and observe him as a curio in Kabir Street, but I had to manoeuvre to get him out of Malgudi hurriedly, when I found that he was planning to seduce and abduct a young, innocent school girl known to me. So there we are, and "finis" on page 116 inevitably.

Why *not* only 116 pages?, I question. While a poet or dramatist rarely exceeds a hundred pages even in his most ambitious work, and is accepted without anyone commenting on the length of his composition, a writer of fiction is often subject to a quantitative evaluation.

The difficulty lies perhaps in classification. *Talkative Man* is too long to be a short story, but is it too short for a novel? I prefer the shorter form, because it gives me scope for elaboration of details, but within certain limits; I can take up a variety of subjects and get through each in a reasonable time, while a novel ties me down to a single theme for at least two years! When I am at work on a novel, I imagine that I am keeping a crowd of characters waiting outside my door, who are in search of their author.

At the beginning of my career I was advised by my literary agent in London to bear in mind that a novel should run to at least 70,000 words, the minimum standard for fiction in those days. The failure of my first novel, *Swami and Friends*, was attributed to its length: "Fifty thousand words are an awkward length for a novel," my agent wrote. A bookbuyer investing 7/6d (in that Golden Age) liked to have his money's worth of reading, I was told. When I mentioned this to Graham Greene in a letter, he wrote back to say, "I hope you will get a subject next time which will run to a full-length book. But that's on the knees of the gods. Only if you see a choice of subjects and lengths ahead of you, do next time go for the longer." A welcome advice. Otherwise, I feared that I might be compelled to inflate my stories with laboured detail and description of dress, deportment, facial features, furniture, food and drinks – passages I ruthlessly skip when reading a novel. While writing, I prefer to keep such details to a minimum in order to save my readers the bother of skipping. Also, I have the habit of pruning and trimming, when I look over the first draft, and then in a second draft a further lopping off is certain, until I am satisfied that the narrative progresses smoothly.

The present work has turned out the shortest among my novels, but if I were to blow it up, I could perhaps push it forward from the point where it now ends, with Commandant Sarasa setting out on an odyssey in search of her slippery husband, across several continents and in many societies and hide-and-seek situations, until she tracks him down, corners him, and finally incarcerates him in the prison of domesticity. Thus I might generate 100,000 words or more and give the volume a respectable girth, fit to top a best-seller list. To achieve this end, perhaps I should acquire a word processor, and learn how to handle it without blowing its fuse or allowing it to outwit me by gushing forth phrases faster than I can spell. But alas, I am not inclined to acquire new skills; I cannot handle any mechanical or electronic device. I have given up even typing, finding the typewriter a nuisance and a distraction when its keys stick or the ribbon gets tangled. Apart from this, still bearing in mind Graham Greene's advice of half a century ago, I do not concern myself with quantity while writing.

I speculate, however, what Commandant Sarasa would say if Talkative Man had advised her to set forth in search of her husband. In her present mood, she would probably retort, "No. Let *him* undertake the pursuit this time when he is finally let out of prison. It will be a long time, though, before that happens. Prison life will have shorn him of his Adolphe Menjou style and his three-piece suit, no woman would even give him a glance, and he will have nowhere to go. At that point he will think of me, but he won't find me. I am going away presently on a UN assignment to a developing country. Your friend won't know where I am gone. Nor am I going to leave my address with you since you are a talkative man and will not keep a secret. The faded Dr Rann, I'm sure, will ultimately seek refuge in your Kabir Street unless he ends up on a footpath in Calcutta or Bombay."